OLIVER KITTEN'S DIARY

About the author

Gareth St John Thomas is the founder and CEO of Exisle Publishing, based in Australia and New Zealand. He has been involved in the book industry since he was 11 years old, when he started helping his dad at David & Charles. Now, his mission with Exisle is to bring books into the world from voices that otherwise wouldn't have been heard, and to give readers something with heart. Gareth has written other adult and children's books including *Finding True Connections, Grandpa's Noises* and *Cats Work Like This*. He divides his time between the UK, Australia and New Zealand.

OLIVER KITTEN'S DIARY

The journals of a mischievous cat's first year

Gareth St John Thomas

EXISLE
PUBLISHING

First published 2022

Exisle Publishing Pty Ltd
PO Box 864, Chatswood, NSW 2057, Australia
226 High Street, Dunedin, 9016, New Zealand
www.exislepublishing.com

A CiP record for this book is available from the National Library
of Australia.

ISBN 978-1-922539-35-9

Designed by Mark Thacker
All illustrations courtesy of Shutterstock, with the exception
of page 192 © Nicky Johnston.
Typeset in Gimlet Text Narrow Light 9 on 14pt
Printed in China

This book uses paper sourced under ISO 14001 guidelines from
well-managed forests and other controlled sources.

10 9 8 7 6 5 4 3 2 1

For Bandicoot

Introduction

My name is Oliver.

Lucy and her mother and father took me away from my mother at the very old men's house. All my family had been living there since before I could remember. Mother told me that she preferred it to the fire engine where she'd lived before, and where I was born. The men had taken us to their home one wild night when we were all being bombed by ice as Mother was teaching us about exploring. Though the old men were always nice to us, they argued with each other all the time, but I never knew what that was all about. They decided to 'put us all up for adoption' and lots of people came along to stare at us. Mother was annoyed as she said she hadn't taught us all she needed to by the time the first of my brothers and sisters went, which was at just five weeks old. They were never taught how to hunt or hide properly, or even climb and fight. Mother told me that I was better at hiding than any other kitten she had ever had – there were dozens of them, but she couldn't tell me about any of the fathers.

When Lucy's family came to the old men's house they seemed friendlier and more genuine than the other people who had been around. Why humans who seem to talk sensibly among themselves get silly and rude among cats is beyond me. What's this 'kitty kitty wah wah' nonsense anyway?

Some of the potential adopters were horrible. 'I was only looking for a white cat,' one of them said. Another didn't think any of us were 'cute enough' and another wanted to know if we could be trained to not meow. A question I couldn't understand was, 'If he's so nice, how come he is still here?' That was asked by a man who waved his finger at me, so I pounced on it and only let go when I saw Lucy coming around the corner. There was a young couple there who also liked the look of me. He had picked me up and seemed to be gentle enough. He then put me down and started talking to the woman with him about litter trays, vets and feeding and 'the importance of routines'. She looked as bored as I was horrified, so I undid his shoelace and had a quick pee well away from the litter box. She laughed and he walked off.

Richard, as I discovered he was called, looked like he wanted to be there and was interested in cats, and seemed to know about us. Unlike some of the other 'husbands' and dads who had been taken to 'just have a look' by their families, Richard didn't stare at his phone all the time and he even hissed at Lucy for doing that. Better still, Richard crouched down and waited for me to come over to him. I felt that I was in control, which made me feel safe. Sophia, Lucy's mother and Richard's wife, left Richard and me alone for a few moments when we first met. This was clever, as she spends a lot of time away at what Richard calls her 'high-powered job in the city'. She knew that when they took me home – which they did – Richard and I would spend much time together.

Richard and Sophia have a son, Lucy's brother Clint. He is only two years old and very unpredictable. Another family member living in the house is Sophia's mother, 'Nan'. Apparently, she 'knows about cats' and her jobs include looking after me as well as Clint and to keep an eye on Lucy. Nan does seem to know something about cats as she made a nice safe place for me hidden behind the lounge with lots of blankets in a basket. I like Nan and I am looking forward to helping her play with the ball of wool that's stuck on her lap.

We all live in a four-bedroom house on the fringe of the city with a promising hunting ground that Sophia calls 'my garden' and I am the only four-legged animal here. That's not counting 'Bubs'.

Day 1

Now that I am six weeks old it's time that I started to keep a journal. Mother said I am a very important cat so I am sure everyone will want to know all about my life. Lucy keeps a journal as well, and as Lucy does almost nothing every day I am sure mine will be the more interesting one. Mother said she would like to know about my life too when we meet up again. I am not a baby kitten any more, I have been playing for half my life already – I can even pounce and I have got the best teeth and like finding my own food, and I've already fought with Richard's fingers.

There is a human baby in the house, and she is almost a year older than me and can't do anything for herself. I think they brought me into this house to guard her. She is called Bubs and as you should know my name is Oliver. Not to be confused with Ollie – a very nice name I am sure, but the naming of cats is a very serious business so please don't call me Ollie. Bubs doesn't know what to call me; she only says three things: 'dada', 'mamma' and 'puddy'.

Day 2

I am still trying to remember everything Mother told me to do as well as not to do. I sometimes become a little muddled, but Mother told me to work hard at things and that they would all come right in the end. For the next few sleeps, I am working on the trouble thing. Mother told me to watch out for it and 'never ever, little one' get into trouble. Trouble should be avoided 'at all costs'. However, as I don't know what trouble is and what it looks like, I am not sure that I can avoid it. Oh, what to do?

Day 3

I spent today looking for trouble. I went into Lucy's room and looked under the bed. There was a big, extra-smelly fluffy thing there that she calls 'Wabbit'. Mother told me that they were good to eat, so I sniffed it and it fell over on top of me. It was big and dangerous, and I had to fight it with everything I had. Wabbit had me pinned right down, and even with all my paws fighting and my teeth biting, Wabbit was still winning. Wabbit must have been making a noise because Lucy got out of bed and that doesn't happen much before everyone else in the house gets back into theirs. She picked me up, told me how clever I was and made me sleep right next to her to protect her from Wabbit.

Day 4

Mother would be proud of me as I can already see that some humans can do things well. It's only my fourth dark night here but I have learnt that Lucy is very smart. She is excellent at sleeping and only gets up to eat and then brings the food back into bed with her. Lucy's mother, Sophia, says that's because she is a 'teenager'. I hope there will be some more of them. I stayed with Lucy all day. It's lovely and warm next to her and she smells nice and knows just how to pat my fur down nicely. Lucy went off for a big, long wash so I came back to my pile of blankets. It still a bit scary around

here without Mother and my littermates so it's good having somewhere safe to go. One blanket tastes particularly nice when I am sucking it and I heard Nan saying that I purr particularly loudly when I have my favourite blanket. That's all very well but I sometimes prefer my own privacy. How would she like it if I commented on every noise she made (and she makes a lot of them – from all sides of her)?

Tomorrow I am going to be looking for some new hiding places.

Day 5

Lucy came and found me after I had just a few hours in the blankets. I am glad she did as the blankets were being naughty. They wouldn't stay still. I had to jump onto one side of them, which is like crossing a huge colourful pond, then pat them down. But they would try to escape on the other side and tangle up into each other. I had to spend hours trying to get them to behave. Lucy rescued me, picked me up and straightened out the blankets and we went back into her bed. That was peaceful.

Lucy's toes tried to escape from the bottom of the bed so I attacked them as fiercely as I could. Lucy shouted her praise of my bravery by yelling my name as loud as she could, and Sophia ran into the room. 'Is everything

all right, darling?' she asked Lucy. 'Urmm,' said Lucy and
picked up her phone. I went and rubbed against Sophia's leg
and meowed at her and she picked me up and put me back
on Lucy's bed. That was obviously where I was supposed to
be. Sophia then went around the room and picked up lots
of glasses, mugs and plates (including those I hadn't had a
chance to lick yet) and left the room.

Day 6

Far too much happened yesterday with the blanket wars
and the great toe fight, so Lucy and I decided we should
stay in bed all day. Everyone else had gone out 'for a drive'
apart from Nan, who announced that she had put a tray of
food outside Lucy's door and also opened the door a little so
I could get out. I came back in after tasting Lucy's food (to
check if it was good for her) and leapt back onto her bed.
Slept for the day and woke up to find Lucy was gone!

Day 7

Being left alone was frightening to begin with but there
were such of a lot of things I had to explore. First, I had to
find trouble so as to avoid getting into it and I also still
needed to find some new hiding places. Bubs has taken
to crawling quite quickly, shouting 'Puddy puddy!' and
trying to grab my tail. I need escape plans. Bubs can't
crawl upstairs so while the blankets behind the sofa may
not be safe anymore I can make bases upstairs. But these
stairs are enormous. Lucy wasn't there to carry me and I

can't leap that high yet. I tumbled down no problem, but getting up was beyond me. There is no litter box upstairs so I can't just move in there permanently. I need to think about all this.

Day 8

Richard has put little gates at the top and bottom of the stairs. He told Sophia they were to stop Clint and Bubs going up and down by themselves. I can squeeze through the bars easily enough but that won't help me much. But I saw Nan open the downstairs gate and leave a pile of folded sheets on the third stair up. It was a big pile nicely overhanging the second stair. I slipped through the bars and used all my strength to leap to the second stair. Then after a little sleep I managed to get my teeth around a single sheet and drag it downwards so I could climb up it. But then all the other sheets decided to fight back and fell on top of me and forced me to the bottom of the stairs. Not fair. I protested and Richard came and picked me up, laughed at the sheets and put me on his lap for the rest of the day.

The new gate Richard put in at the bottom of the stairs fell down and Sophia came into the kitchen holding it, waving her hands about and shouting at Richard.

Day 9

Clint was trouble today. He found a ball and started kicking it in the house. I hid under the sofa when Richard picked him up and told him that balls were for outside. Clint screamed about that so Richard took him outside and I went to check on Bubs. It's clear that Nan's ears are not any good as she slept all through Clint's rage, but Bubs was awake and worried. Bubs and Clint live for some of the time in big cages in the nursery room, rather like we did at the shelter. I walked around it to where Clint was leaning against the fence. He obviously wasn't very happy there. Unlike the ones at the shelter, his cage only had two walls and was propped up against the playroom's back wall. By my dabbing at one of the corners and Clint pushing we created enough space for him to crawl out. Now we had teamed up, we went into the kitchen together. We had fun but rather a lot of things fell down and we left the kitchen after a while as everything was so messy.

Day 10

Things felt a bit different in the house today. Even Richard didn't seem quite so caring, so I waited for Lucy to come into the kitchen and made a big fuss of her when she arrived. She took me upstairs with her. We found a great new way of travelling: she has food and drink in both her hands and I am wrapped around the back of her neck, navigating. We ate all the food and then slept all day.

Day 11

It was a busy morning as I had to wash Lucy's hair and face, as she is obviously not old enough to do it properly herself. Then I had to get some revenge on that ball-mad Clint, so I rushed out in front of him when he was running and shouting down the hallway. He tripped and fell over in a big noisy heap. Well, the humans were distracted so then I visited Bubs to discuss her escape plans, but they had securely closed off her fencing so she will have to jump out. I cannot yet jump in to show her how, but I am growing and we can do that soon.

Day 12

Richard has put a baby gate in front of the kitchen door. It's too narrow for me to squeeze through so I jump over it and land on a nice slippery surface. It's fun to watch the humans' faces as I whizz into their most important room, getting all their attention at once. Clint cannot get into the kitchen by himself so I like showing off to him that I can. Richard likes to carry me though and climbing up him is a real adventure – he is very tall and doesn't have much hair so his head is nice and warm.

The new kitchen gate fell down and Sophia just waved her hands at Richard but didn't bother shouting this time.

Day 13

Sophia took me to the vet today. It was the first time I've left the house. She put me in a box with a handle and a little gate to look out at the front, and we went in the car that had brought me here. Fortunately, Lucy came too, otherwise I would have been terrified. Nasty, smelly dogs were everywhere, along with some poor distressed cats. There were things in cages that looked and smelled like they might be prey. Birds, turtles, mice, rats as well (I didn't know that they went to vets), and there also were hamsters there. When I am big enough to go hunting away from home this might be somewhere I want to come — the dogs seemed too upset to be dangerous, and distracting people might be easy. I wondered what the point of a gerbil was.

The vet was obviously so impressed with me that she wanted to admire everything. My mouth, my skin, my eyes; she even rubbed my tummy and asked Sophia to leave a sample of my poo. Odd, these humans.

Day 14

It looks like I am in trouble again. Sophia came back late last night from work and tripped on my nice big wool trail. Then she shouted about mess everywhere and shouted at Richard for 'not being able to manage two babies and a kitten'. I thought Sophia needed cheering up so I jumped on her lap to purr at her, but she spilled her drink. I started to lick it off her clothes but that sent me straight to sleep. I awoke on my blankets when it was cold and dark. I was lonely and hungry, so I had to wake Richard up to feed me and then Lucy to keep me warm. I needed to check on her as well, as she needed cleaning again. But Richard came in, picked me up and said something about too much energy for my own good and put me on the blankets. I must get some new hiding places.

Meantime, it's time for sleep but I will just move that wool around a bit first.

Day 15

By the time I was awake Richard had already come back from shopping and was destroying the back door. I asked him what he was doing but he just fed me. So I must use those questions again. But then he got noisier and noisier with the door and I fled upstairs. I can jump them easily now and over the baby gates. Lucy let me in and I went to sleep.

Richard knocked on the door and took us both down to meet the 'cat flap'. This, they told me, was going to be a life-changing event. Richard has put a very big Oliver-sized door within the door and all I have to do is jump in or out of it as I please. I am saddened by this. I am not yet three months old but the humans are already trying to get out of one of their key responsibilities – opening doors for me whenever I want. So I am pretending not to understand how it works.

Day 16

My tail keeps following me around. It's annoying when a kitten wants a bit of privacy. So today I decided to chase it away. It's cunning. I caught it a couple of times, but it bit me, so I had to let go. Being a natural hunter, I was fully absorbed in the chase so was shocked when Richard suddenly picked both me and Tail up and put us through the cat flap. I was there in the hunting grounds. My tail and I decided to work as a team and Tail helped me balance over the log crossing the stream, and we bravely prowled into the woods.

The hunting grounds are enormous. It will take me

forever to have everything organized. They are very noisy too. Tail and I were extra careful, but we were spotted by those big, fat, ugly black and white birds that try to sound like ducks. They chattered away and one of them landed right in front of us and looked me straight in the eye, asking what I was doing. How rude. It was much bigger than me and it tried to peck at Tail, so I had to run home to keep Tail safe.

Day 17

Have been thinking about that bird. I think it's what Sophia calls 'a damn magpie'. Tail and I need to show it who's boss. But that might be difficult; for a start, like all birds it doesn't play fairly and can fly away when it wants to. So, we need to find a way of stopping that. I thought Sophia could help as she obviously doesn't like them either. Sophia was in the garden, so I found her and went to have a chat. She had a little wheelbarrow full of straw she was putting around the plants. But when I got there she was busy

digging a hole for another plant. So I went to sleep in the wheelbarrow but was rudely woken up by her screaming in surprise when she picked up a big handful of straw and found me slipping out of it. 'Richard, what's your damn cat doing in my wheelbarrow?' she shouted. Richard didn't answer so I went off to inspect her new plant. Humans are as rude as magpies.

Day 18

As Sophia was no help with the damn magpie, I decided that today I would see if I could push Lucy out of bed long enough to show Magpie that I had big friends and that Tail and I should be treated with 'respect'. But Lucy didn't get out of bed. So I didn't either, and that was a perfect day.

Day 19

I thought that I hadn't seen enough of Clint or Bubs and they would probably need supervising for the day. I found them both in Bubs' cage, with Nan sitting in the fat chair watching them. I jumped onto Nan's lap and let her tickle my tummy and play with my ears for a few minutes before going to sleep. When I woke up there was something new to be investigated. From the ceiling right over the cage someone had hung a group of pretty items that moved round and round just out of Clint's reach. Clint was trying to hit them with his toy spade and Nan kept on telling him, 'Don't hit the mobile Clint, that's not nice.' But he ignored her. Oh, the possibilities for me were so many and it was so exhausting thinking about them all that I went back to sleep.

Day 20

It is the weekend and last night Sophia decided it was time for a family dinner. Normally, everyone, including me, in this household eats separately but tonight Sophia put us all together. Bubs and Clint were in their special chairs with Nan between them, and Lucy was pushed out of her bed to join us with her phone and sat between Sophia and Richard. They didn't leave a space for me on the table. In fact, they don't want me on the table at all and Sophia got upset whenever I jumped onto it and firmly but gently put me down.

The cloth Sophia had put over the big table has big tassels at the four corners to play with. One of them fought back and hit me on my nose so I bit it and tried to tug it off. I was winning and was taking it somewhere where it would be easier to bite through its neck and the whole cloth was coming with me. But then Sophia suddenly shouted 'Stop!' and a few empty plates crashed onto the floor. How she made that happen I don't know, but both Clint and Bubs thought it was funny. But I was in trouble again.

Day 21

Finally, I had a serious day finding new hiding places. I did well. There is a cosy space behind the dishwasher I can squeeze into. In the laundry area there is a big, warm cupboard with a hidden dark bit at the top. I dragged some of Sophia's clothes that were drying there up with me and had a nice sleep to test it all out. But when I woke up, they had closed the door.

Day 22

Asleep in the cupboard.

Day 23

They finally opened the door. I didn't answer Nan's question, 'What are you doing in here?' but just ran. When I came back, Richard picked me up and put me on his lap in his office. He was working on his computer and needed me to help bash what he called a mouse. Humans are very confused about mice. They take them to vets and get them to help work their computers. Mice are to be chased, organized and sometimes eaten. Richard clearly doesn't know much about mice, so now that I am nine weeks old, I will try to catch a real one so he can see what they really are.

Richard went to make coffee and the 'mouse' got out of hand. It had to die. But then I thought it might be just a little over excited, like Richard says happens to Clint. So I tried to pick it up and put it behind the bookcase, but it just beeped at me. Cheek! No matter how hard I swotted it wouldn't stop until Richard put me back on his lap for a sleep. I don't think Richard is incredibly happy with me. I will get him a mouse tomorrow.

Day 24

I checked in on Bubs first thing this morning while sitting on Lucy's neck. Bubs was awake and had thrown her little rubber teething thing onto the floor. So I jumped down, picked it up and put it back in her cot. Bubs threw it out again and Lucy picked it up and wiped it a little before putting it back. Bubs threw it again, so I ran off with it and hid it. Silly baby. Bubs started to scream, and I, having had enough of these humans, went through the cat flap back into the hunting grounds. Tail was up and we were after mice. But Clint was outside kicking a ball, so I stopped to look at him. Maybe I could get him to kick it at the magpies. But he kicked it at me instead and I had to leap out of the way and stalk him for my own safety.

Day 25

Sophia was home all day today working on a 'special project', which meant she was in the office and everyone had to be quiet. Richard and I went out into the hunting grounds, and I showed him just how good I am at climbing trees. Up and up I went, branch after branch. There were some birds that were most annoyed, but I just kept going — I would deal with them later. I stopped on a big branch and turned around to look at Richard admiring me, but he wasn't there, or I couldn't see him, and it was a long way down. Well, it certainly was a good place to hide, and I could see right across the woods. That's when I got a big shock. There was another cat, an excessively big, ugly grown up putting her scent on what should be my territory. I meowed and meowed in protest, but she didn't hear me.

Mother had told me that you are supposed to pretend to get stuck in trees. That way you get a lot of attention from humans and that's how I came to be born in a fire engine. But there was no time for that today. I scuttled back-first down the tree and leapt off the last branch in pursuit of the invader. But it must have seen me coming as it had run away in fear before I got there.

Day 26

Sophia was still at home on 'her special project'. She was obviously working too hard, so I went and had a nice long chat with her. I told her all about the naughty magpies and the extra enormous invading cat she would have to deal with. But she didn't seem to mind much and I know now that getting rid of monsters is yet another of my responsibilities.

I liked being with Sophia. She had tied her hair up with some nasty ribbons, which I was able to undo with my teeth, and she told me that I was very cute. I found another place to hide, behind the big computer screen; it's very warm and a good place to sleep.

Day 27

This was supposed to be a hunting day, but Bubs wasn't happy. Richard called it 'the middle of the teething problems' and she was crying all morning. I jumped into her cot while Nan was asleep and tried to lick her better. Bubs quickly went back to sleep and so did I, and when I woke up Richard had taken Bubs for a bath. I joined them and had to fight off the plastic ducks that threatened to surround her. I don't like getting wet, though, so I had to dab at them from the bathroom stool. That stool has a nice cork top, which is great for scratching, so I am claiming that stool as a place for me. If anyone else is sitting on it, I will have to sit on them; and if anyone leaves anything on it, I will have to push it off into the bath. Richard left his coffee mug on there so into the bath it went and Bubs didn't like that and screamed. For a moment Richard couldn't imagine what Bubs had done.

Day 28

Everyone has gone and left me alone today and I couldn't make up my mind as to whether I should stay in and guard the house or patrol the hunting grounds and get rid of that invading monster and bring Richard a real mouse. Mother told me that I can't do everything all the time so I found a compromise, which was to go to sleep all day in Bubs' empty cot. That way it was nice and warm for her when she came back. I even licked her little rubber mouth things clean (apart from the one I left in the fireplace).

Day 29

Now everyone is back home it's time I had a decent amount
of attention. Lucy is always lovely and gave me a little kiss
as she let me out of her bedroom, and as Sophia and Richard
had left their door ajar I jumped on their bed with them.
They didn't seem to notice so I patted down the piece of
pillow that was showing next to Sophia's head. 'Oh puss,'
she said, so I nuzzled into her face and licked her. She
patted me and lifted me onto Richard's chest. There were
a lot of big hairs waving around there. I didn't like them
much so I came up with a brilliant plan. Making sure my
claws were fully retracted I looked adoringly into Richard's
sleepy eyes as he went back to sleep with me on his chest.
I purred away for a while and when I was sure he was sleep
I selected the longest hair to tug on. I was ready to pounce
but Clint woke up crying and I had to rush off and rescue
him instead. That plan will wait.

Day 30

There was a new and extra powerful smell in the house
today. It was coming from the kitchen and I had to get there
immediately to taste what it was. It was called 'fresh fish'
and quite rightly Richard gave me some, and seconds as well.
I have never tasted anything so good in my long life. It was
a blissful experience — so much nicer than the mushy stuff
that comes out of a tin. If I had known fish tasted so good,
I wouldn't have left the two red ones in the bowl alone as
much as I have. Now I must plan how to capture them without

getting wet and preferably without knocking the bowl over. That's going to take some thinking about.

Day 31

It didn't work. The fish are still alive in the bowl. The bowl isn't broken but it went all over me, and that traitor Lucy was much more interested in rescuing the fish than poor nearly drowned me. At least Sophia gave me a nice patting down with a towel, even though she was muttering something to Richard about 'your flaming cat'. I am going to try again — fish tastes too good.

Day 32

I decided that I'd better be extra cute for these humans. If they can bring fresh fish into the house, I need them on my side. Mother told me about something called a 'charm offensive' so I tried very hard today.

I gave Lucy an extra lick this morning and a kiss when she put me outside her room. Then I went and had a chat with Nan, who was just off on her motorbike. I sat inside her helmet to warm it up for her and licked her face too. Richard was in the kitchen making breakfast for everyone else. The normal gunk was in my bowl so I rubbed my whole length up and down his lower leg and purred at him. He crouched down to say hello and I clambered onto his neck, which he liked, and kept me there for several minutes before I jumped down to purr on Sophia's lap while she was drinking coffee. Sophia seemed happy enough and was quite pleased when I snuggled up to her ear then fell asleep back on her lap. Later I went outside and pushed the smaller ball towards Clint, who rolled it back and we tried to go back and forth for a while, and I didn't run away when he tried to grab Tail. I even hopped into Bubs' cage and helped her go back to sleep. Sophia and Richard crept in when I was there and Sophia even said to me, 'What a cute cat.' Job done.

Day 33

They all went out and left me alone again today, which was quite distressing as there was much for me to look after all by myself. Perhaps they went out to find fish, so I thought I would do the same. But someone, and I think it was Sophia, had put the goldfish bowl on top of the bookcase and way out of my reach. For now.

I went into the hunting grounds. I stayed low and quiet and then a thin, long, extra dangerous snake slithered menacingly across a paving stone. It must have been at least a quarter of the length of the whole stone. It stopped, obviously confident in its super strength and clearly not having heard the name of Oliver. It took courage but Tail and I leapt towards the snake, taking it completely by surprise. I bashed it with my right paw and leapt into the bushes before it could retaliate. Seconds later I was watching its next move when that horrible magpie picked up the snake in her beak. Tail and I were furious, and I leapt like a tiger across the bushes right onto the horrid bird.

Magpie was terrified and she dropped my snake and flew off, making lots of idle threats. I picked up the snake and strutted back into the house and left it on the doormat for everyone to see. I thought I had killed it, but it must have escaped as all Richard said was that he wondered how a worm had got into the house.

Day 34

Everyone was home today, so to be fair to all of them I had a turn at sleeping on all their laps. Except for Clint – I slept on his head, and he didn't seem to mind – and Bubs and I played running races instead. Bubs was crawling quickly, but I still let her win, though I wish she wouldn't try to lift herself upwards by pushing on my back.

Day 35

A big box arrived with new clothes for Sophia. She left the paper on the floor, and it rustled at me, so I went to war with it. It took me all morning. The paper kept on breaking up into smaller pieces and floating across the room and by the time I had leapt on those and destroyed them several others had escaped, and the battle continued. Sophia came in at the end and she must have been terribly upset about her new clothes as she looked so unhappy that I had to hide in the box. Had a long sleep there.

Day 36

As soon as I woke up Tail and I decided to have a race around the house upstairs and downstairs. We went around five times before Richard diverted us, so we ran straight into the hunting grounds. Richard came along as well and tried to catch up with us. But I pounced on his feet and Tail brushed his legs, so he gave up and sat on the old bench as we whizzed around the garden. We then stalked him from behind and leapt on his lap as a surprise. He picked me up and held me close to his face, saying, 'What are you up to little kitten?' So I gave him a lick. After sitting on his shoulder, I saw a very cheeky yellow flower waving at me in the breeze. I pounced on it, bit its head off and brought that into the house for Lucy, who seemed perfectly pleased with it and put it in her hair. I thought she looked lovely and it was very reassuring to have my hunting skills appreciated.

Day 37

One of my favourite places is sitting on the windowsill overlooking the hunting grounds. It's so interesting that I can spend at least five minutes being still there. Today I spotted where the magpies nest and I ran around the tree several times, so they know I am onto them. Noisy, cheating, snake-stealing rascals.

Day 38

Clint and Bubs shared a bath today and that required a lot of supervision. First, I had to make sure that those flows of water, hot and cold, went where they were supposed to. I bashed at them a little, so they knew that I was in charge. Then I had to push Nan off my stool (she had obviously

forgotten the rule) and then I had to dodge Clint's splashes. Nan was busy mopping them up with a towel.

I find water endlessly fascinating, but it gets my fur wet and I don't like that at all. While Clint was busy splashing and Nan mopping, I found a long chain coming out of the bath, so I pulled at it and while I wasn't looking all the water started to escape. 'It will be your turn next!' said Nan, so I jumped onto the sink and out the window into the hunting grounds.

Day 39

Yesterday, as I was jumping out the bathroom window, I thought I saw another cat looking at me. I went back to have another look and it was still there. It copied everything I did. I moved my head, and it did the same; Tail swished at it and the cat's tail swished right back. It didn't seem aggressive, so I put out a friendly paw and it did the same. I jumped up and the other cat did that too, but I fell off the sink and I think it stayed where it was. That cat doesn't smell at all and makes no noise. So I went to tell Lucy about it, and she was brushing her hair and there was that cat again. I leapt but he disappeared. It was all a bit odd, and I got tired just thinking about it.

Day 40

I had a lovely night sleeping with Lucy. She is the most perfect human. Today she had Henry, a friend, arrive and because Lucy told me all about it first, I wasn't very scared. Henry is even older than Lucy and he stared right at me, which I thought was very rude. As he was Lucy's friend I ignored his bad manners and made sure to sit on him. Even though he put me down several times I always jumped back onto him, especially when he was trying to brush Lucy's hair with his hand.

Sophia must like Henry a lot, as she came in and out of the room several times, once without knocking. One of the times she asked Henry if he would stay for dinner and though he said yes Richard came in fifteen minutes later to check. Henry turned on some ghastly noises he called music, which I found very scary and had to run up Lucy's neck and jump from there to hide beneath the curtains. Fortunately, Sophia came back again, and I was able to run out the door. But I was worried about leaving Lucy alone with stroking Henry so I yowled outside her door and she let me back in. But the music was too loud, and Sophia let me back out again. Then I had to do it all again.

The third time I came back into the room Henry's toes had freed themselves and were moving across the floor towards me. I pounced on them and managed to get my paws around a big one. It wouldn't stay still so I bit it. Lucy laughed so I bit it again. Henry became even ruder, asking Lucy, 'Why can't you control your silly little kitten?' She was about to answer when Sophia came in to say their

dinner was ready. Lucy followed Sophia out the door and
Henry closed it with me inside.

Well, I had to go somewhere, and he had shut me in on
purpose, but I didn't know I could pee quite so much as I did
on his jacket. I thought he might not like it, so I left as soon
as they came back after dinner and went into the kitchen
myself, and then went and hid in the laundry cupboard.

Day 41

There was no sign of Henry today.

Day 42

I think I might have upset Lucy, so I went out into the
hunting grounds to capture something special. The magpies
are still too big for me. I have already tackled snakes so Tail
and I were after mice. I knew they were there. They are very
smelly, and we soon found a hole that seemed suspicious.
But I wasn't totally sure what a mouse looked like. Richard
and Nan roll a little ball towards me with a bell inside and
tell me to 'go catch the mouse' but there was nothing like
that to see. Mother had occasionally brought home some
dead things and I was told that they included rats and mice,
so I knew I would recognize one when I saw it.

While Tail watched out the back, I put my paw down
the hole, but it didn't touch anything. I put my face into
the hole, and I was purring so loud with excitement that it
echoed back on me and I couldn't hear anything in the hole.
I backed away and hid behind a large bush to keep watch.

Tail and I had only been there for two minutes when we heard a noise. There were some people coming towards us across the grass. I had to keep low, so I couldn't see their faces, but they were barefoot, and one set of toes looked so familiar that I had to pounce on them. Henry screamed and Lucy laughed louder than I have ever heard her laugh before. I allowed Lucy to give me a quick pat and I gave her a kiss. Henry didn't look at me at all, which was a good thing as perhaps he is learning manners.

Day 43

I have started exploring a bit more near the house and found that if I climb up the tree near the garage I can jump on its roof and see everyone coming and going. This is going to be an important space for me, so Tail and I carefully chose a sitting spot. A blackbird sitting on the roof was startled by us and started an enormous amount of chatter. Tail said that was to be expected when a famous snake killer and toe biter moves into a new position.

There was not much happening for ages, so I was pleased to see Richard and Nan walking towards me. Richard stopped at just the right place so I jumped on his back, to save all that climbing. But all he said was, 'Just as well I am wearing a big jacket today'. He didn't say anything about it being a wonderful surprise to see me. I shall have to surprise him again. Nan was very nice though. 'Where did you come from Mr Oliver?' I like it when she calls me that — it makes me sound even bigger and more important than I feel when all the birds fly away in fear of me.

Day 44

It was cold and wet outside today, so I stayed indoors and patrolled the furniture. There were some interesting things to explore, and a few mysteries remain. Sophia and Richard have their own bathroom and there was a cat like me in there, but like the others it quickly disappeared. But underneath the sink there is a cupboard containing some interesting boxes with strange smells coming out of them. Needing to get a better look, I pushed a box onto the floor and there were some little tube things in there. A few of them started pouring out powerful-smelling liquids; they reeked so much that I had to jump back onto the sink to escape. And there I saw it. On a ledge above the sink there was a very big tin that smelt just like Sophia. I clambered up and saw that the tin had lots of holes in it and signs of powder inside.

Tail and I had a discussion. We knew we were in trouble. The place was stinking us out and we couldn't get out of the bathroom without getting wet and we really don't like that — especially with such foul-smelling things. So we hatched a plan. Tail swiped the tin with holes in it so it fell forwards, and with my right paw I bashed it towards the pool of smelly stuff so that the powder inside covered it up. It worked, a little, and Tail and I escaped in decent shape. But I had to spend the next three hours cleaning myself. It was quite the longest grooming session I have ever had to do.

I had only just finished cleaning myself and Tail when Sophia walked in. She picked me up firmly and took me back into her bathroom. She then put my face near the

smelly pool and said several times, 'No cat! No cat!' I tried to wriggle free, but she wasn't letting go. Sophia had gone mad. It was obvious there was no cat there, but I don't know why she had to tell me and bend my whiskers at the same time. After Sophia put me down, I had to spend another hour grooming. It's tough being a kitten around here.

Day 45

It was still cold and wet today, so it was another day of exploring in the house. Tail and I decided to stay clear of Sophia and her bathroom — one was crazy and the other stank.

Richard had opened a hole in the top floor's ceiling and there was a funny little stairway going up to it. There was no sign of Richard, but Tail and I went up anyway.

There is a whole new floor I wasn't aware of up there.

We had just carefully walked into the big, dark space when a mouse ran out in front of me. Tail and I leapt on it, and I had it in my mouth, but as I tried to get a better grip it slipped away and ran right to the other end of the floor. We were after it in a flash but it double-backed on us and ran down the stairway into the house. We went after it but going headfirst down those stairs was not a good idea and I slipped through a gap and just managed to avoid falling the whole way by hanging vertically, supported by my front legs. I meowed loudly, and Richard shot up the stairway quicker than the mouse had raced down it and rescued me. Richard must have seen the whole thing, as he put me down and pointed to where the mouse had gone. I rubbed against his legs to say thanks and followed the trail. But even the smell had gone. So I went back to the funny staircase to wait for the mouse to come back. Lucy picked me up and asked why I was sleeping in the middle of the hallway and took me back to sleep with her.

Day 46

There is a mouse in the house. It has to go. This is my chance to show just how necessary a kitten I am. The first thing to do is to find it again. Richard had put the ladder away and closed up the hole, so that floor was closed. I was thinking about investigating coming at it from the outside when I decided I needed a rest. I went and talked to Nan, then had an extra-long chat with Clint and Bubs. I helped Clint develop his ball skills and let Bubs win a crawling race again.

Those sparkling moving things (I think Nan called them 'a mobile') still intrigue me so I am going to have to get a better look.

Day 47

I was out in the hunting grounds today when I spotted the big cat I had seen there before. She is very grown up, and put her mark on my territory. I followed her and put my mark next to hers in the hope she gets the message.

Day 48

It was Lucy's fifteenth birthday today. I cannot imagine being so old, but Mother had told me that she knew some cats who reached over 20 human years. I hope I live at least that long. Lucy had a big cake, which didn't taste very nice and it messed up my whiskers.

There were a lot of boxes covered with paper — Nan called them 'presents' — and even Sophia was home for teatime to watch me help unwrap them all.

Birthdays are important to cats. I am almost twelve weeks old, which makes me around four human years old, so I am closer in age to Clint and Bubs than I am to Lucy.

Lucy looked extra pretty today so I sat on her and purred most of the time. She seemed happy, too; she is always happier when she is not spending all her time looking at her phone. Unwrapping her presents was fun. I managed to get paper everywhere but there was one big paper bag that swallowed me. I couldn't see anything, I had no idea which way was up or down and Tail was absolutely no help whatsoever. (Between you and me, I am worried about Tail.) Anyway, I fought and fought and pushed the murderous bag right around the room and eventually clawed my way out of it and bit it to death. Everyone there clapped me, even Sophia, who was laughing. I thought that might have been a bit rude. No one should laugh at a cat.

Day 49

One of Lucy's presents is extra super special, and she is sharing it with me. It's like a big table that she puts right across her lap in bed, and it has room for her computer, our meals and me. It also has a pocket for her phone. I found out that when I scratch on the table the phone falls out onto the floor, and when Lucy is not looking I can push it under the bed, with all the other horrible things, and she doesn't use it for a while.

Day 50

I spent the day on the garage roof and saw Sophia drive off to work. Nan went off somewhere on her noisy motorbike and Lucy went into the garage, grabbed her bike and wheeled it outside. That had possibilities. I meowed at her to say hello, but she had earphones on and couldn't hear me. Then I realized that nobody was looking after Bubs or Clint. I raced back indoors and zoomed into the playroom and saw Bubs was fast asleep. But where was Clint? I was very upset and meowed and meowed and all of a sudden Clint appeared from nowhere and patted me. 'There, there, puss,' he said, which I thought was very grown up. It was great to see him. But where had he been? It was all a bit stressful for Clint too, so we went into the playroom and found somewhere to sleep.

Day 51

As usual I slept overnight with Lucy but was woken up by
Sophia asking her if the little ones had been okay and to
thank her for looking after them. I didn't say anything but
thought I should make a little distraction, so Tail and I
rubbed against Sophia's legs. I looked up at her and meowed
so she picked me up, and I gave her a kiss and snuggled into
her ear. She had a long, bright, dangly thing hanging out
of it — I don't know why they call them rings — I dabbed at
it but it tried to move away quickly so I dabbed at it again.
Sophia laughed and said something about 'a daft kitten'.
But Lucy came to my rescue. 'Mum, will those earrings be
safe with Clint?' she asked. The distraction was complete.

Day 52

Back on the garage roof, I saw Lucy get onto her bicycle and I
was sad to see her go. But then I had an idea. There is a little
enclosed basket tied to the front of the bicycle. If I could get
into there I could go out with Lucy and keep her safe. I would
feel safe, too, as Lucy always takes great care of me. But I
had to let her know that was the new plan.

I waited till Lucy came back and said hello to her in
the garage as she dismounted, then I leapt onto her seat.
Lucy was pleased to see me, and I rubbed her hand and she
tickled my ears. Then to her surprise I looked at the basket,
meowed and then looked at her and meowed. 'There is
nothing in there, darling — just an old shirt,' she said. But
I meowed again — so Lucy put me in the basket. 'You look

good in there, puss. Maybe we should go for a ride one day?'
Then I purred louder than I ever have before so Lucy knew
that I liked the idea, but we both agreed that it was time to
get food from the kitchen and go back to sleep.

Day 53

Richard was up on the very top floor again today and I
went up the ladder to see if the mouse had returned. It
had – with a whole family, and the place stank of them.
This was going to be trouble. But then I heard Clint crying
downstairs and Bubs joined in too. This was a problem. I am
not good at thinking about things for long; I am too busy for
that. But either I had to be the responsible hunter keeping
the house safe, or the main carer for the little ones. I told
the mice that I could see them, and they should stay where
they were and await instructions. I then carefully went
downstairs. Tail helped this time and I zoomed into the
playroom.

There was chaos in there. Clint had managed to hit the
mobile with his spade, and it was barely holding together.
Bubs had fallen over the toy box and was crying while
pointing to the broken mobile. She was very afraid of it.
Lucy was on her way, and I could hear Nan was coming too
but there was no time to lose. So I leapt onto the mobile to
finish the work Clint had started. But it wouldn't give up. It
went round and round with me on it and that's when Sophia
joined the others and said something about 'that naughty
kitten'. Not fair. I went and sulked in Lucy's bed for the rest
of the day.

Day 54

Spent the whole day sulking in Lucy's bed.

Day 55

Spent the day sleeping in Lucy's bed.

Day 56

Spent the day sleeping in the laundry.

Day 57

Tail and I were keeping watch from the garage roof when Lucy came to pick up her bicycle; we were in the basket right away. I said hello but Lucy couldn't hear me with her earphones on and I don't think she noticed me until she had mounted and off we went. This was so exciting. Of course, the bicycle is a lot slower than I am, but it felt very scary and wobbly, and it was windy too. I managed to climb up the shirt and look over the top of the basket at the road ahead. Gosh, there was a lot to see.

As we left our avenue, I saw that cat that keeps coming into my territory. I thought she would be impressed to see a bicycle-riding, toe-biting snake killer but all she said was, 'Whoa, hang on tight there, young fellow.' Then a big black animal came running towards us making a ridiculous noise.

'Go away, doggie,' said Lucy and pedalled faster, but it

almost overtook us and its face was getting close to me. Mother had taught me how to deal with these things and I got ready to bash it on the nose. But Lucy rescued me first. She suddenly stopped the bike and shouted, as loudly as her mother, and the dog went away.

We carried on riding. I guarded the bicycle when Lucy went into a shop, and I watched all the people and cars. A few clever people stopped to admire me. One of them was about to pick me up when Lucy came back, and he thought better of it. 'We will have to get you a collar, Oliver,' she said. The ride home was exciting too, apart from cars like Sophia and Richard's going past and leaving nasty fumes and smells everywhere.

Day 58

I have decided to deal with those mice on the top floor once and for all.

Day 59

Slept. Can't remember where.

Day 60

Mice are boring. I prefer bicycles. Spent the day waiting for Lucy to get on hers but by the time she had got up and finished painting her face it was already too dark to go out. I think she always looks beautiful. Like all these other humans, even Bubs, Lucy is very big but it's a pity they have to change their skins most days. I just groom mine. Very carefully. Lucy tells me that I am a good-looking cat and, of course, I believe her.

Day 61

I am getting bigger and so is Tail, who is getting both longer and bushier. The thing I find amazing is that I have white socks. They are the only part of me that is white, and I cannot understand it. I look at them for a long time every day but how they came to be white is still a mystery. If I ever see Mother again, I will ask her. But she might not know. She was never clear on who my father was.

Day 62

I was attacked by a small bird — Lucy called it a 'moth'. I was sitting on the windowsill when it fluttered up from the side and started scratching my ears. I tried to dab at it, but it flew a little bit above me. The moth escaped while we went back to sleep. But later, after Lucy had got up and put the ceiling light on, the moth brushed past me and tried to attack the light. I climbed up the wardrobe with the open door and went from shelf to shelf with just my front paws and started dabbing at it. But clothes were falling onto the floor, so Lucy and I agreed to work together.

Lucy picked me up and moved me right up close to the light. She held me tight, and I boxed the moth to the ground using my left paw. Once it was down, I pounced on it. Moth didn't taste as good as fish, but I enjoyed hunting it and will try that again. On second thoughts, maybe moths aren't a kind of bird because they only seem to wake up at night. I gave Lucy lots of head bumps after that.

Day 63

Richard said he wasn't feeling very well today. I think he must have been working too hard, so I climbed on his lap then snuggled up with my left ear on his chin and my two paws pinning down his right elbow. He had to stay exactly where he was and we both slept for hours. It was a hard job for me, but Richard needed the rest. I only woke him up when it was time to feed me. I needed to keep a good eye on him so when he went for a small walk around the garden I went along, too. He sat on the bench, and I kept guard and chased away a pesky blackbird. I think Richard was grateful for that. When he went back inside I followed him and gave him a good grooming. He obviously hadn't washed behind his ears for weeks and they needed a lot of attention. Then his fingers — ew! They were dirty too; no wonder he wasn't feeling well.

I had briefly walked into the playroom to check on Bubs

and Clint when Richard called me back. He had just fed me so I would normally have ignored him but he clearly needed me so much that I meandered gracefully into his office. He wanted to play, and I had to pretend to be interested in a large paper and metal contraption, which looked like a replacement mobile for Clint and Bubs. So I bashed at it and it instantly fell to pieces. There is just no helping some people, so I left him to it and went to find Lucy.

Day 64

Richard came back home and called me to him. He gave me a present to thank me for looking after him so well the other day, He called it Fish and it smells like one too. I don't think it's a real fish. I jumped on it and it chattered loudly at me. Its head reared up, so I jumped away and came around the back of it, but it moved again, making lots of noise. I had to jump on its head again and then it rolled over and became even nosier and flipped itself around on the floor.

Lucy came in in the middle of the first fish fight. 'Ah Flippity Fish, nice one Dad!' she said and tied a ribbon to the naughty fish and started walking away, dragging an increasingly noisy Flippity along the floor. I chased it and even though Lucy sped up I caught it with both my front paws. I turned it over and thought that I had killed it. But it was just pretending to be dead.

I was just taking the smallest nip to see what it tasted like when it flipped up its head and started talking and bouncing away. That was scary, so I hid behind the sofa until Lucy picked me up and took me to bed.

Day 65

We had a visitor today. Tail and I were on the garage roof when we saw her arrive. She had a big, noisy vehicle with an enormous door on the side. She opened the door and took out a big, brown package and rang our doorbell. I know how all that works. Lucy never hears it because she is either asleep or has headphones on. Richard hopes Nan will hear it and Clint and Bubs don't think it's any of their business. Nan normally doesn't think it's any of her business, either. So I had plenty of time to investigate. There were a lot of other packages in the vehicle, and I was sniffing at them and thinking about jumping in when the driver came back. 'Hello cutie,' she said, and I immediately liked her so gave a little jump up beneath her hands and she liked that. So we had a nice chat for a while until Richard came out.

'Ah, I see you have met our security cat,' he said. Richard saying that made me feel enormously proud, and after passing bits of paper around, Richard picked up the parcel, the driver patted me goodbye and she drove off.

'Come on guard cat, let's go and have a look at this,' said Richard. So I followed him into the house and helped him open the parcel. It turned out to be yet another new mobile for the playroom. No doubt I would be testing it out soon enough, but the box was brilliant – just the right size to sleep in and stretch out a bit. I tried to move it from Richard's office to behind the sofa where my blankets are, but it didn't seem to want to go there. But Nan, who had joined us, knew exactly what I wanted to do and carried it there for me. I must pay more attention to Nan; she knows about cats.

Day 66

Lucy was fast asleep when I was desperate to get out this morning. Only the little window was open but I managed to climb out of it and onto the ledge. Above me was a long pipe coming all the way from the roof — and it was surrounded by little legs. Mice! I edged my way up there and saw that the mice had made a small hole behind the pipe into the top floor. The hole wasn't big enough for me to get into and I didn't want to get stuck. So, reluctantly, I clambered back down and banged on Lucy's window to let me in. She never heard me but Nan did and asked, 'What are you doing there, you daft kitten?' and gave me a kiss. I spent the afternoon on Nan's lap helping her with Bubs and Clint.

Day 67

At first, I thought he was ugly. A hideous, noisy, slobbering dog. He was in the driveway on a lead with a girl talking to Lucy. I saw them from the garage roof. I was so pleased to see Lucy that I stood up and meowed at her and the dog saw me and started barking. What a racket. 'Shush,' said the girl and Lucy called me down to 'meet the puppy'. Reluctantly, I came down.

His name was Bear but, as I discovered, he was not very fierce. And, as I also discovered, not as hideous as I first thought. Bear told me that the girl's name was Bella and that she and Lucy had been friends forever. But now they lived a long way away and Bear was only here on holiday for a few days, staying with Bella's aunt.

Bella and Bear came into the house, and he started running all around my territory, so I chased him, and we played with each other. He is twice as big as I am but about the same age and he is not as fast. Bear jumped at me, and I leapt over him and dabbed his ear.

They didn't stay long but I was pleased to have met a puppy. These humans, especially Lucy, are all very well but they don't seem to do very much and spend most of the time just sitting down.

Day 68

Bear came around today with Bella, who went into Lucy's room, so Nan took Bear to meet Bubs and Clint. I don't think I want to eat Bear and he promised not to eat me, and I think we might even become friends. As soon as we entered the nursery Nan said to Bear, 'Sit pup' and he immediately sat. I thought it was amazing that Bear did what he was told. Cats wouldn't do that. Nan stayed with us all the time, and other than Clint thinking Bear might be a horse to ride we had a lot of fun. Bear and Bubs played ball and I made a few leaps at the new mobile, which made Bear excited even though it was too high for me. Bear said he couldn't jump that high, either.

Bear put Clint's big ball, which is larger than me, in front of his face and pushed it all over the room and into the safety pen, which then fell over. Dogs are so clumsy.

Bear wouldn't leave me alone for very long; he sniffed and pawed and played nonstop. Nan saw what the problem was and picked me up and carried me to my special place

in the laundry cupboard and closed all the doors so I could sleep in peace.

I do like Bear, but he is exhausting. However, now and again he will just sit down and immediately fall asleep without grooming himself first — and he doesn't even groom when he wakes up. I will have to teach him how to do that. If I do that for him, perhaps he will chase and bark at the magpies for me. Those birds will be even more respectful of me when they see that I have a big dog friend.

Day 69

Bear's going back home tomorrow, and I'm going to miss him. He was brilliant with the magpies. I told him all about the problem and he raced around the hunting grounds barking at the magpies and everything else in case they had ideas, too. He then left his mark where the territory-invading cat leaves hers, and he even went to sleep on my blankets, so I was able to groom him. Something was very muddled, though, because after he left there was a new blanket in the pile that smelled very much like Bear and one of my blankets had disappeared.

I tried to show Bear my special place on the garage roof, but he can't climb so I went up there and watched him run around the hunting grounds. Bella came out and gave Bear new instructions like 'stay' and 'go down'. Tail and I thought it funny that dogs would do this.

Dogs don't seem to have any manners at all and need to be told how to do everything. Bear even tried to squeeze himself through the cat flap but got stuck. He only went out backwards when I leapt at his face.

Once back in the house, Bear immediately ate everything in my food bowl in less than a second. He then drank some of my water and spilled the rest all over the floor and promptly started playing again. Bear has no idea about 'please and thank you' and cleaning and washing before and after meals. And simply taking my food was silly. I don't think it was nasty, though. Bear doesn't think much about things and is much more instinctive than I am. He would have seen food and thought, 'food: eat quickly; water: drink now'. Whereas I know to look very carefully at what there is to eat, sniff it several times – and make sure it is dead before even thinking about eating it.

Fortunately, Lucy saw what had happened and fed me some extra nice food last thing tonight, but I was a bit shocked by Bear's ill manners. I am going to have to teach him a lot next time we meet. Bear needs to know about grooming, only going through doors after they have been opened for him, not to slobber, only to bark at naughty people and birds, and not to eat or drink any of my food. I am sure there will be more he needs to learn but that's all I can think of for now. Oh, being polite would be a good idea for him as well. That might be a bit difficult to understand and Bella will have to teach him about that.

Day 70

Lucy stayed in bed all day. I got up as far as her windowsill and frightened away a little waggy-tailed bird that was sitting outside without my permission. Had funny dreams about being chased by Bear with the ball in front of his nose.

Day 71

I had escaped from Lucy's room using the small window again and was waiting patiently for her to wake up to let me in. But Lucy forgot about me and left for school. So, I was on the windowsill all day before Nan came and found me. I wasn't very happy at all. Nan must have told Clint because when I saw him, he pointed his finger at me shouting, 'Shut out, shut out, shut out!' I am going to have to do something about that child.

Day 72

Tail and I were back in our usual place on the garage roof, peacefully minding our own business as usual when a large vehicle drove up, like the one the big parcel had been delivered in. But this vehicle smelt of fish! Unfortunately, the driver took out just a small parcel and closed his door. I immediately went to say hello to him, rubbing myself against his legs and purring and meowing, when Richard came out and collected the parcel and invited me into the house. I then had to watch Richard take out a lot of delightful smelling fish, and only give me a plate-sized portion before ruining the rest of it by covering it with lemon juice. These humans just don't understand food.

Day 73

Bubs and I had our first proper chat today. I have no idea what she said but she seemed happy enough. I just purred away, and Nan didn't mind me grooming Bubs.

Day 74

Sophia was home in bed all day coughing a lot. Richard says she has been working too hard again. But I never see Sophia doing anything, so I can't understand how. However, I made sure Sophia did even less than usual today by pinning her to the bed and licking her every time she tried to make a move.

Day 75

Sophia seemed a little better today and was very pleased to see me and patted me everywhere. She even found her extra-special comb and made my coat much softer than usual. I didn't think that was possible. I like it when Sophia is not well because at least she does something useful.

Day 76

Lucy and I were in the hunting grounds today when a furry, brown animal at least half my size ran at high speed in front of us. What cheek! I gave chase. Lucy told me it was a rabbit.

The rabbit had such a long head-start on me that I couldn't quite catch it before it went down a hole. I managed to get partway into the hole, but it suddenly turned sharply left and I was stuck for a while before Lucy pulled me out and called me a 'daft kitten'. That wasn't fair, but I gave her a lick anyway because she is always extra lovely.

Day 77

Tail and I went back to the rabbit's hole and waited and waited. But it didn't come out. We waited some more. I was waiting so stealthily quiet and crouched down so very low that I went to sleep. It was dark and cold when I woke up. There was no moonlight, and the only sound was the owls.

So there we were, brave Cat and Tail alone in the dark jungle when we saw a big shape move very close to the hole and start sniffing at it. What was this monster? We will never know because Tail lost his nerve, turned around and shot us back through the cat flap at high speed.

Day 78

After such a big adventure yesterday, I needed to sleep today and found the perfect place for it behind the dishwasher. It was quiet there for a while and then the machine started humming and spluttering, and its tentacles began throbbing. I grabbed one of its pipes and pushed it and bit it and pushed it some more, but then it suddenly escaped and spouted cold water over me. Outrageous. I had to rush to Lucy to complain about it. She just went back to sleep.

Day 79

Lucy carried me downstairs for food and found the kitchen floor was sopping wet and Richard was mopping water. Sophia looked suspiciously at me. Richard explained that a pipe had come out of the dishwasher and they were lucky that he had found it in time or the whole house could have been flooded. 'Dad,' Lucy told Richard, 'it couldn't have been Oliver, he was with me all night.' Lucy is lovely. I made a note to give her extra kisses but as we went upstairs together I saw Sophia shaking her head.

Day 80

Early today there was a new male's voice in the kitchen. Tail and I went to investigate. The man who owned the voice was wearing what looked like a bed sheet with lots of pockets and holding what looked like a very big spoon with the end missing where it goes into your mouth. He must have been talking to himself as there was nobody else in the kitchen. But he had attacked the dishwasher and had dragged it into the middle of the room, and was hitting the back of it with his big spoon. So I went up to his ankle and bit it. It's my job to defend the house and that includes the machines. But the big voice man didn't see it that way as he threw his spoon-like thing at me, which missed and smashed right through the pantry door. '@#*** cat!' he roared.

Day 81

Decided I'd better hide today as I might be in trouble.

Day 82

I am in trouble. Nobody is looking at me except Lucy.

Day 83

Hid in case I am still in trouble.

Day 84

Lucy came back to her room with some fresh fish for me.
The world is marvellous again.

Day 85

Tail and I went to find the rabbit hole. But somebody or
something must have moved it because we're sure the hole
is not where it was, and we looked all day.

Day 86

Found the rabbit hole and had a nice sleep by it. Couldn't
remember why Tail and I were there, so we went back
indoors.

Day 87

Lucy put a collar on me today. It's very pretty. 'We should
have done this ages ago,' she said. Now I am much more
grown up and less likely to get it snagged on branches
or anywhere else, so it's a good time. The collar is bright
red, and it's got a buckle that can come undone if I need it
to. There is an impressive-sounding bell to announce my
arrival and a little silver disc telling everyone who doesn't

know it yet what my name is and both Richard's and Lucy's phone numbers.

This is exciting — it means I can go anywhere I want. When I want to go home I will find someone who likes cats and all they have to do is call one of the numbers and either Richard or Lucy will come and pick me up. Perfect. The collar is a bit smelly; Lucy told me that it killed fleas and I would get used to the smell. I hope it works. I don't like fleas at all — there were a couple of mobs of them near the shelter and I don't want to see them again.

Lucy said that now I had a collar I could come back out in the bicycle basket with her and that's very exciting. I will be with my favourite person, favourite anything in the world — that's Lucy — and seeing lots of exciting and interesting things and showing off my new collar. It's thrilling. I do hope I can sleep tonight.

Day 88

This morning finally came and Lucy (after many headbutts, licks, meows and kisses) finally woke up. We had breakfast on her lap desk and I managed to hide the phone again so we would have all the morning — just Lucy, Tail and me — to see the world.

Lucy and Richard were having a chat. 'I have written out a list of a few things we need,' he said, handing Lucy a piece of paper and some money, and off we went. Lucy had made up the basket nicely with some empty bags for me to sit on and a small towel. I noticed she had added another basket at the back of the bicycle, so I didn't have to share my space with the shopping. She is so clever.

Lucy carried me into the hardware store and put me in one of their trolleys. We were about to start looking for nails when a nasty woman wearing what looked like a blue sheet shouted, 'No cats allowed here.'

'Where does it say that?' asked Lucy.

'It doesn't say that,' said the woman, 'but they are not allowed.'

'You don't know that,' said Lucy, 'and how long have you worked here?'

'Three weeks and they shouldn't be allowed.'

'You don't know much, do you?' said Lucy and we went past her.

'Oh great, a cat! Just what we need,' said another woman in an identical blue sheet. 'You couldn't leave him with us for a few hours, could you? We just cannot get rid of the mice and none of the products we sell for that actually work.' This woman was called Meredith. She reached over to me, read the name tag on my collar, and asked, 'Do you want to help us out Oliver, please?' I purred and gently headbutted her hand.

Lucy said we would try to come back tomorrow afternoon but I was rather booked up until then. 'That's great,' said Meredith. 'Now, what were you wanting to buy in here?'

That evening, Richard and Sophia seemed amazed that Lucy had managed to get so much from the hardware store, far more than was on the list and because of me it was all free. But, as Richard pointed out, I have never caught a mouse in my life, so I am either going to have to learn very quickly or get some help. Or even hide, but I decided against that as it would let Lucy down.

I went outside looking for the cat that trespasses in my territory and, sure enough, I found her near the rabbit hole. I am a lot bigger now than when we first met so she was quite polite. I explained that I needed her help, and we agreed to meet at the hardware store. The cat, called Lolly, didn't know there were any mice there and seemed excited about it all.

Day 89

As the light was beginning to fade we cycled back to the store, this time to the big rolling door at the back. Lolly was already there and a friend of hers came too, but he didn't want to be introduced. Meredith was waiting for us and was pleased to see us. 'Oh, you have some friends with you,' she said, and let us all in. 'Feel free to go home,' she said to Lucy, 'and come back whenever you think that the cats have had enough time.' Lucy and I were both worried – she had never left me alone before and I am still quite a young cat. But I pretended to be much braver than I felt and sprinted through the door, running right to the back of the enormous room. I ran up and down and there were dozens of mice. They were terrified to see such a fast, fierce cat as me.

As I ran up to the back of the big storage area some mice ran to the front and Lolly and the nameless cat chased them outside. By then it was fully dark and Meredith had not put the lights on. But the mice could see us perfectly well and there were lots of cheeky little eyes looking at us. Lolly took

charge and told me what to do.

I ran around the store going as far back as I could while Lolly followed me, going slowly. Lolly was on one side of a big aisle and Nameless on the other.

'There are rats here too,' said Nameless. 'It's going to take us all night and then some, and Kitten here can't keep on doing zoomies or he will be asleep in a minute. We need another approach.'

Lolly didn't say anything, but she was looking at me. I said that I had better find Lucy and tell her what was happening in case she hadn't already gone home.

I couldn't believe that Lucy would have abandoned me so quickly, and sure enough she was at the entrance holding her bicycle and speaking with Meredith. Just as I came out Meredith rolled down the big door. Perhaps Nameless and Lolly were trapped. 'Don't worry about them,' said Lucy as she put me back on the bicycle. 'They are very grown up.'

Day 90

I saw Lolly in my hunting grounds today and went to see how her night went. She told me that she and Nameless had a very busy night herding the mice outdoors. Nameless had some fights with very big rats and really enjoyed himself. So much so that he had accepted Meredith's offer of a full-time job as the hardware store's pest control officer. There were blankets, litter trays, water and occasionally biscuits and treats as part of the pay package. Nameless had asked Lolly to be his assistant.

Lolly had come to say that she wouldn't be in the hunting grounds for a while. She also told me that I would have to do something about the rabbits otherwise there would be too many of them but, if I liked, she and Nameless would come and help me deal with them one night. I said that I didn't think that would be necessary but that I appreciated Lolly letting me know she was finally leaving my hunting grounds. We thanked each other and, true to her word, Lolly left the hunting grounds. I watched all day but there was no further sign of her.

Day 91

As I have been focusing on important things in the big world, I was worried that things at home might have got out of control. Or, worse still, that someone might have forgotten me. So I spent the day asleep just in front of the bathroom door so everyone at home knew I was there.

Day 92

Nan must have been doing some tidying up recently. All my blankets have a new smell, apart from the one Bear left behind and my box that the mobile came in has gone. Nan must be in one of those moods as she threatened to give me a bath today as well. So, I went back to the hunting grounds to talk to the rabbits, but they were being shy again.

Day 93

Nan tricked me this morning by throwing the ball with the bell in the bath, so I had to chase it up and down and round and round and it kept getting away. I was so busy that I didn't notice she turned the water on. I have had several baths already but always just in the sink. I had seen Lucy and Richard having showers in the bath lots of times. Once Richard asked me to bat away some naughty water that was coming out of a tap too quickly and I have rescued both Clint and Bubs from the ducks. So Nan must have known that I was ready for the big cat's bath.

But the water was just too wet and I had to escape by climbing up onto the shower's shelf. The shelf collapsed and fell, with me and everything on it, into the bath. Nan fished me out, saying that we would have to try it later.

I don't think so.

Day 94

Everyone had to dash out of the house this morning. They didn't say why but nobody looked very happy, and they packed suitcases with them. I tried to get into Lucy's, but she wouldn't let me stay in there. I am sure they will be back soon, so I am just going to sleep until they do. Then I might see if I am big enough to get to the goldfish bowl.

Day 95

There was a stranger in the house, and she was in the kitchen. I crept downstairs and saw that whoever she was had the good sense to change my litter and put food and water in my bowls. Then she left again. It cannot be all bad, but I don't like being alone, especially without Lucy, so I just slept.

Day 96

Today the stranger was back. She changed my food and things over again, so I thought I'd better say hello. I was very polite. The stranger stinks of rotten fruit and the stuff that Sophia pours into her glass all night that makes her voice go funny when she shouts at Richard. Still, I rubbed my myself against her legs and she seemed happy.

Day 97

Richard and Lucy came back, yeah!

Day 98

Richard and Lucy are gone again, this time with more, bigger suitcases. Before they left, Lucy told me that Richard's mother had fallen in her big house in the country and that she had asked them all to come down to stay and look after her. But they needed me to guard the house. The fruity woman was 'a cat-sitter' they hired 'from the agency' and she would be moving in for a week or so.

So, they have abandoned me to a smelly person. Not happy. After they left I ripped up a chair and that made me feel better.

Day 99

Fruity person is here now. I am hiding.

Day 100

Still here so I am still hiding. Ripped up another chair. If they are not back it will be curtains tomorrow.

Day 101

Today I was seriously worried. I love my family, but they've been away a long time now. Fruity woman doesn't play with me and just left the curtains I pulled down on the floor so I will get the blame for it.

Day 102

At last, they are all back. I can sulk now, and I am especially annoyed with Lucy — how could she just leave me? An innocent little kitten and all. I am going to ignore her for a week.

Day 103

Spent all day with Lucy. Sophia came in to ask where all the wine was but otherwise — apart from Richard asking where his brandy and whisky bottles were and Nan wanting to know what happened to her beer and cider — we were left alone.

Day 104

Richard has a new toy, a light, and needs me to help him play with it. I know it's him using it but we both pretend I don't know that. Humans are like that: they don't know that I am happy playing. Richard's light is a lot more fun than a mouse and I only have to pretend to kill it. It is an extremely fast light. It attacked my white socks at first and

I leapt upon them, which almost tripped me up, and then the light escaped onto the wall. I pounced but it had moved again and was on Sophia's hair. I think Richard was being naughty.

The light then moved right across the carpet and I just had to get it, but every time I was on top of it, it just moved a little further way. Every time. I sped up but so did the light. Then it took to hiding underneath a chair and inexplicably disappearing before suddenly coming back near the top of the goldfish bowl. I started climbing up the bookcase to get there and easily found it, but the light had gone back to the carpet, so I leapt backwards onto it to loud applause from everyone in the room. But the light still escaped. Now it was on the curtains, and I was getting ready to leap when it moved into the kitchen and onto my food bowl. Cheek! I stopped to eat all the food so it couldn't hide there again and had a little sleep on Lucy's lap.

When I woke up Richard was still there, but I saw that the goldfish bowl had been moved. Clever man, but I will find them. Anyway, moving the bowl created a good, high, safe spot for me, right in the middle of things. So that's where I spent the night.

Day 105

Nan is so kind. She put the box from the mobile on top of the bookcase and rolled a blanket inside it. I now have the perfect place to hide, watch and sleep when I want to be on my own. But that is not very often, and I have been alone far too much recently.

Bubs is crawling and sort of walking at high speed and Clint is getting bigger and nosier and just runs everywhere and into everything. I tried to calm him down by tripping him up on the carpet then headbutting him and purring into his ear. Sometimes I sit on his back and then he takes me for a ride through the downstairs of the house, and he likes that. Bubs chuckles a lot every time she sees me and seems happy most of the time. But Bubs is just cute; she can't do anything. I have been taking her some food because she cannot get her own and she likes that — or would, if Nan didn't always take it away from her first.

Day 106

I went to sleep thinking a lot about some unfinished business. Those rabbits are breeding too much and I need to have a word with them. Those cheeky goldfish are going to be fun to hunt and even eat, as I haven't had fish in ages. Finally, those mice on the very top level still need to be driven out. So, there is a large amount of work for me to do. It's also time to see how Lolly and Nameless are getting along.

I am going to start with the goldfish. Richard feeds them every day so all I need to do is keep an extra close watch on him and he will lead me to my prey. Richard likes me draped around his neck so I will spend all day there tomorrow. Just in case Lucy gets jealous, I will give her some extra attention tonight and re-plait her hair when she is asleep.

Day 107

I remembered my plan and draped myself around Richard's neck and hung around him all morning. He was happy about it and it was lovely being close to him. We were in the office, then the garage, we took a cup of coffee to Sophia and had a chat with Clint and Bubs, and helped Nan cutting wood. But there was no sign of the goldfish bowl. If Richard wasn't going to cooperate, I was going to have to find the prey by myself.

I started by walking along the top of the kitchen shelves. They weren't hiding there but I did find a few things that obviously shouldn't have been there, so I pushed them gently onto the floor. They made quite a good noise so I pushed some other things too, but then thought I should look elsewhere. I looked in Clint's room and managed to leap on top of the wardrobe. It was far higher than Clint could ever reach. But it was crowded up there, with lots and lots of empty, fruity-smelling bottles covered by blankets. So I pushed everything onto the floor and Richard and Sophia came running, and very quickly they were pointing at the bottles and shouting at each another. Nan came in and they started shouting at her. It was terrible and then Lucy came

down. Well, I can't stand anyone being nasty to her, so I stood in front of her and threatened everyone. Lolly taught me how to do that — all I have to do is make myself look super big by arching my back upwards, with Tail standing as high as he can go. Then I hissed. Everyone stopped shouting and looked at me. It worked. Nan put Clint down and gave me a quick pat before rushing off to check on Bubs. Everyone else hugged and all of them patted me at the same time. 'Clever Oliver for finding our bottles,' said Sophia. 'That so-called cat-sitter must have put them there.'

'Yes,' said Richard, 'he has been hunting them all morning by the looks of the kitchen.' Even Sophia smiled.

Now I was in Sophia's good books again, I thought I could risk going back into their room and bathroom. And when I made it to the bathroom, that's when I saw it ... Yes! They had put the goldfish bowl on top of their bathroom cupboard. This was going to be easy. But then Richard called me from the kitchen and, as I ran out, Sophia closed the door. I quickly looked back, and I realized that she knew what I knew. Stealth would be required.

Day 108

Lucy talked to me a lot last night, saying that I was her best friend ever. I know that and she is my best friend, too, like Tail is but a bit different. Then Lucy said that Henry was coming to the house tomorrow and could I be nice to him too, please? I was thinking about that and feeing sad that I might have to share Lucy, when Clint banged on the door shouting, 'Nan, Nan, Nan!'

We rushed out and it looked as if Nan must have tripped going downstairs and, only having two legs, she fell badly, with one of them pointing the wrong way. I have not seen a human leg look like that. Nan was making very quiet, unhappy noises. It was just Nan, Clint, Lucy and me in the house, but I knew what to do. I leapt down to lick her leg better and Lucy got on the phone and passed it to Nan, who looked pleased and spoke to someone.

Moments later there was a knock on the door and two identical-looking strangers rushed inside, acting as if they were with animals at the vet. They pushed and prodded and put something on Nan's face, and eventually put her on a contraption and carried her out the front door. Lucy and I followed; the men had a special vehicle with beds inside, and they laid Nan on one. She looked sadly at me so I jumped in right next to her. They closed the doors and we drove off at high speed.

One of the two men must have been driving because the other was in the back with us. He ignored me altogether but paid Nan a lot of attention and soon Nan stopped moaning, smiled at me and gave me a pat.

Everyone ignored me when we arrived at the hospital. They took Nan out of the van while she was still in bed — I was impressed they had beds you could be carried around in. I would like that. They left the back doors open and I jumped out to follow Nan. Just then a big police dog spotted me. It tore away from its human and came rushing towards me. I zoomed into the hospital and up one flight of stairs, through many doors, and then ran into an open cupboard. I think I lost the dog, but someone closed the cupboard doors. It was quiet and dark but comfortable, so all I could do was go to sleep.

Day 109

Suddenly light came into the cupboard and a lovely lady all dressed in blue picked me up and said, 'What are you doing here sweetie?' I gave her a headbutt; she seemed very nice. She picked me up and looked at my collar. 'Oh, so you must be Oliver,' she said. 'Let's call your mummy, shall we ?' and she carried me into a little kitchen and gave me some milk before taking me to an office. I sat on her lap when she called Lucy's number. But Henry answered.

Had they lost a cat called Oliver? she asked. 'No,' he said, 'never heard of him,' and he ended the call. I heard it all. I was shocked – that nasty, nasty boy, now he had Lucy to himself.

The nurse then called Richard's number. He didn't answer but she left a message. 'You are not really supposed to be here, you know, but if you are quiet, we can just wait for your dad.' I purred, gave her another headbutt then hid underneath a chair and went back to sleep.

Day 110

I woke up and there was a line of men with lots of papers in their hands waiting to see the nice lady. But then Lucy arrived and jumped in front of them all, picked me up and whispered, 'You are not supposed to be here, Oliver, which is why all these forms need to be filled out. This is a hospital you know.' Lucy hid me in her bag, and we went off to find Nan.

Nan was still in bed next to a lot of other people also in bed, in a huge room with a very slidy floor. One of Nan's legs was propped upright and encased in something white. I jumped out of the bag and gave her a kiss and she was very pleased to see me. 'I am going to have to be here for a few days, Oliver,' she explained, 'so you will need to look after Clint and Bubs for me.' Then Richard came in and started talking to Nan, so I used the opportunity to introduce myself to some of the other women in the room and they all seemed very pleased to see a cat.

Someone said there was a 'therapy cat' that came once a week and spent his time in the hospital visiting just about everyone in there. That might be quite a good job, which I think I would prefer over being a pest control officer. It is very hard to decide what I want to do when I am grown up and I know that Lucy is dealing with the same questions.

Day 111

It was good to wake up in Lucy's bed this morning. It was so comfortable that I decided to stay there all day.

Day 112

I was thinking about the possible job as a therapy cat. Lucy told me that I would have to be at least a year old before I started but that's not much more than six months away. But no one has said anything about what my pay and conditions would be. At least you get litter trays, blankets and some food and treats as a pest control officer. I decided to go and find Lolly and see how she and Nameless were progressing with their job, and to tell her about my new opportunity.

Day 113

Lolly wanted to know if I had met any therapy cats and suggested that I find her or him when I was next at the hospital but Nameless didn't approve at all.

'Rats, mice, vermin — they are cat's business, young Oliver,' said Nameless. 'You don't want any of this human care stuff. You can't trust humans, you know. You will make friends with someone in the hospital and the next day they will be gone, without leaving any token of thanks. Stay away from humans. At least there will always be vermin to deal with; you can trust them to be there, you know. I used to live with humans. Big family it was and all. They had a girl, like your Lucy but not as pretty if you don't mind me saying so. It was all very homely, but they were more interested in their telephones and televisions than each other, let alone me. Then one day they all packed up and left. They even took my carrying basket, but I wasn't in it, was I? Oh no, they didn't want me where they were going, did they? Just left me behind to fend for myself after three whole human years with them. Can't trust humans – but vermin, now there's a future in them. Cat's got to have a career, son, you are right there, but don't have anything to do with humans. Vermin is as vermin does.'

Lolly said she could take or leave humans and that she could stay in quite a few of their houses when she wanted to. But they were a bit noisy and the food they provided was very rarely fresh enough and she didn't like watching television or seeing them looking at their phones all day, either.

'Yes, vermin, that's the thing,' said Nameless. 'You will be wanting to get rid of that collar and bell, though. They will be laughing at you from minutes away if you are wearing that. I can tell you how to get rid of it if you like: all you need to do is find a wall with an uneven bit sticking out. That's easy enough to do; humans don't seem to be able to build anything straight nowadays, do they? Then just lift your head up and rest the right-hand side of the buckle against the uneven bit and move your head rapidly to the left — really fast and hard, mind, like you just saw a rat — and it will come right off.'

I thanked Lolly and Nameless for their advice and told them that I was looking forward to seeing them again.

Day 114

Today was a shocking day — so awful that I am not going to talk about it.

Day 115

Yesterday I went to the vet, and they have now made it impossible for me to breed. They didn't even ask me. Sophia took me. She has three of her own children but isn't going to let me have any. I think Nameless could be right about humans. I am tired and sore. At least Lucy is kind and is staying right next to me. She told me was she was sorry she didn't come to the vets but said she would have found it emotionally difficult. Huh, emotionally difficult! What's that got to do with it?

Day 116

Asleep.

Day 117

Sulking behind the sofa.

Day 118

I am feeling better, and Lucy gave me lots of fish. Nan hasn't
come home yet, though, which is worrying. We mustn't
forget about her.

Day 119

Lucy played with my collar today and added something to it
that she called a leash. A cat on a leash – that's a daft idea. I
ran into the hunting grounds and found the garage wall and
did exactly what Nameless suggested, and the collar and
leash came right off before Lucy had a chance to catch up
with me. Then I ran off to talk to the rabbits.

Day 120

The rabbits were being cheeky, if not rude. I had already
told them that they were breeding too much but they hadn't
taken any notice, had they? They said that at least they
could breed, which was obviously more than I could do

nowadays. I thought that was very unkind.

Three rabbits came out of the burrow and ran around in mad circles. 'Catch me if you can cat, catch me if you can cat,' they taunted as they ran away. Other rabbits nearby joined in and then a very big rabbit indeed came toward me and then turned and waved its disgustingly big backside at me. That's just as rude as a rabbit can be.

Lucy came and picked me up and asked if I wanted to go to the shops with her. But she had the collar and leash in her hand so I jumped away and ran off to see if I could find Nan on my own.

Day 121

I had only been to the hospital in the van or Richard's car. I knew it was quite a long way towards the afternoon sun, but it was much further than I thought so I had to stop for the night.

That's how I got kidnapped.

Day 122

The man was perfectly polite at first. He said hello respectfully and invited me in for a good dinner and showed me outside the back door for a few moments and let me sit on his lap a little bit. He smelled a bit like fruity cat-sitting woman, but I didn't mind as I wasn't going to stay there for long. But it was warm, and I transferred to a comfy chair with a cushion and fell asleep. He was there when I woke up and I thanked him for dinner, said I was in no mood for breakfast but thanks all the same and waited by the front door for him to let me out so I could be on my way.

'Oh no you don't, puss, you are staying here,' he said, and he picked me up with very strong hands and put me in an upstairs room and closed the door. I yowled and scratched but he didn't take any notice.

'Shut up, you horrid ungrateful cat!' he shouted, sounding as loud as Nan's music. I was terrified and shaking but recovered my wits sufficiently to think of a plan. I knocked a vase off the table, and it smashed noisily on the ground. The man came running into the room. I rubbed myself against his legs as if I was very pleased to see him and was very sorry about the vase. He left the door open and I followed him downstairs, making friendly meowing noises. He picked up a dustpan and brush and then I meowed plaintively near the back door as if I need to go out for just a minute. The man opened the door and I slowly walked out, with him watching me. Then suddenly I shot into extra high speed and leapt clean over the garden wall. All the man could do was shout but I wasn't listening.

I was in a big park, which I recognized as being close to the hospital. I thought I would have to be super stealthy to get in again without being spotted by the uniformed guard dogs, but it didn't look possible. So I walked straight towards one of them with brass buckles and silver pips on his harness coat. He was a senior-looking officer guard dog and I told him that I was the new therapy cat and asked what the best way in was. 'Follow me right now,' he said, and he took me straight through the front door and instructed,

'Three floors up, third on the left and then second left. Quickly now, and you will need a pass for tomorrow.'

I found Nan and she was very pleased to see me. She telephoned Lucy to tell her I was there. I was too tired to do anything other than sleep, hiding at the bottom of Nan's bed underneath the leg that was pointing at the ceiling.

Day 123

Lucy woke me up and took me home in her handbag. Nan came too, holding onto some big metal bars she called a frame. I jumped out at the front door so Lucy could help Nan walk down the ramp. The guard dog saw me. 'You have done well young cat, getting that one moving. I thought she would be in for another six days, and you put in overtime on your first day. You have a bright future here. Well done. Now hurry them along, will you, there are people waiting.'

Day 124

Sophia was back home and said she would be here until Nan was fine. This required a bit of reorganization as Richard's computer was moved into the kitchen and Sophia moved into the office with hers, and closed the door and vanished all day. So, Lucy and I had to look after Clint and Bubs. First thing we had to do was get Clint ready for preschool, as he will soon be three years old and there is going to be a birthday party to prepare for.

Lucy dressed and fed Clint. I put what I thought would be useful in Clint's bag, including some of my biscuits,

Sophia's pen, purse and notebook, and some other things that had been left on the table and were easy to push into the bag, including bread, all of which had been left on the kitchen table. The doorbell rang and one of Clint's friends was parked there with his mother ready to take Clint to preschool. But there was a dog in the car. I don't like dogs being outside my house without my permission, but rather than make a scene I went to bed next to Bubs and made sure she slept for a few hours.

Day 125

Richard moved me into Lucy's room and I slept there all day and all night after she came back from school to feed me.

Day 126

Lucy didn't want to go to school today. She said that the new art teacher was 'a bit suss' and the English teacher was 'a real dope' and that her 'squad is all split up now'. None of that sounded very good so I meowed sympathetically and snuggled up close to her face and gave her a good licking. 'I knew you would understand,' she said and got dressed.

After breakfast I walked her to the bus stop and came home to see that same dog as yesterday in the car that Richard was putting Clint into. The dog saw me and started barking and I just walked calmly past, with Tail wagging at the dog. But if he comes again there will be trouble.

Day 127

He came again and there was trouble.

I was walking Richard and Clint to the door and the car was already there with the door open, and the dog came running out, barking at me with his big jaws open. The dog was at least three times as big as Bear but not as polite and not as well dressed as the officer guard dogs at the hospital. 'Oh, Jacques, stop that and get into the car this instant,' said Clint's friend's mother, and Richard roared at the dog and tried to catch hold of it, only just missing. Tail and I escaped up a tree and waited till they had gone. An hour or so later Richard came outside with Bubs and asked me if I wanted to come down.

I had been very scared, but Richard had done all he could, so I allowed him to make a big fuss of me for the rest of the day, right until Lucy came home and he told her how brave I had been.

Day 128

I discovered that I could climb up the curtains and walk across the rail at the top and slide down safely by holding on tight as I am going down. It was great fun doing this until Sophia came in and wagged her finger at me to stop. What is wrong with that lady?

Decided that this should be cheer-up Sophia day. I killed a flower in the garden and dropped it on Sophia's face to wake her up. She just grunted. I then plaited her hair while she slept. I don't think that she noticed. I washed behind her ears (well, it doesn't look as if she ever does that herself) but Sophia didn't appreciate that either. I then just sat on her chest and purred, and Sophia went back to sleep and seemed happy to see me when she woke up. So, Sophia is just tired all the time, especially with Nan being out of action for so long. I gave her lots of extra kisses, and she did seem to cheer up.

Day 129

There was a lovely big family fish dinner tonight with everyone in their places around the kitchen table. Sophia didn't even mind me sitting on Lucy's shoulders or sharing her fish. Richard said that as the holidays were coming up very soon we were going to rent a big house in the country and spend some time there. Oh no – I thought they would send mad bottle-hiding, fruity-breath woman from the agency to feed me. Or leave me alone as people had done to Nameless. But Sophia said, 'Oliver must come with us. We need him as much as any other member of our family.' That made me so happy that I walked right across the table onto her lap, and everyone clapped.

We will all be going at the end of next week, once Lucy is back from school.

Day 130

I like the idea of days with a special plan — and today was revenge day. After I had walked Lucy to her bus, Tail and I formed a plan. We had stayed up late with Nan and Richard watching gymnastics on the television. So, we were ready when the same car driven by the same woman with the same Jacques turned up outside to pick up Clint.

I made sure Jacques saw me as the car pulled up and then Tail and I climbed onto the garage roof. Sure, enough Jacques came bounding out the car and was immediately asked, 'Oh darling, do please stop that', which of course he took no notice of. But Jacques could not climb up to us and went round and around in circles, barking in front of the garage. We made the best gymnastic calculations we could. Tail and I leapt onto Jacques' back then pirouetted right off it onto the tree trunk and clambered well up until we'd found a safe place to watch the reactions.

It was all so exciting that I am going to have to tell you the rest tomorrow, but now I am going to sleep with Lucy, who told me I am the bravest, fiercest kitten cat there ever was and I deserved lots of extra fish. I told Lucy that she was the best girl there ever was. After I'd reminded her a few times to get me the fish.

Day 131

I couldn't help thinking all day about how things had worked out so well yesterday. After Tail and I had leapt onto

Jacques, the lady driver shouted at Richard asking, 'Why can't you control your cat?'

'He is just defending himself from your dog,' Richard shouted back.

Meanwhile, Jacques climbed back in the car and was whimpering in shock. The woman then suddenly drove off, leaving Clint behind.

Sophia came out and looked at me in the tree. 'Nice one, Oliver,' she said. Sophia must have seen the whole thing and was as annoyed about that silly dog as I was. I jumped in Sophia's car as she drove Clint to his preschool. I now know to remember as many details as I can about places (I might need to return there one day) so I had a good look around from the car's front while Sophia took Clint inside.

Day 132

Yesterday I saw Sophia coming out of Clint's preschool building talking and laughing with Nicolas's mother — the woman who has that mad dog, Jacques. Treachery. I hope that doesn't mean Nicolas is coming to Clint's birthday party at home tomorrow as that means Jacques will probably be coming too.

Day 133

Jacques didn't come to the party today. I was the only pet there, but Clint's friend Roger had his mother, Lydia, with him and she had a guide dog. The dog told me to call him Echo. Nicolas was also there and seemed very wary of me. He knows how fierce I can be. It was good to see that the right message was being passed around the neighbourhood: don't mess with Oliver, he is a tough cat!

Echo was offered as much attention as I was, and in my own house! But I was not very jealous as he is a wonderful animal. For a dog. Lydia told everyone that Echo preferred not to be patted as it distracted him from being a working dog who keeps an eye on everything. But Echo told me that he didn't mind; looking after Lydia was quite easy as she had quite a bit of sight left and he had plenty of time to play.

Roger dropped his plate on the floor, but Echo picked it up without anyone else noticing. Echo was always watching and caring. When we were playing pass the parcel he took it upon himself to bark, just once each time, which was the signal to stop, and none of the children argued. I encouraged the children by chasing after the parcel as well. Everyone had brought a present for Clint, and I helped him open them ... and that's when the trouble started.

I had plunged into a pile of wrapping paper, checking it was empty and trying to tidy it up a bit, making sure everything was dead and in properly small pieces. I was very absorbed and hadn't noticed that the whole room had gone quiet. I came out of the wrapping paper to see that there was a fire on the table! I couldn't see where it was coming from. I looked at Echo, but he was facing elsewhere listening to the children who were singing 'Happy Birthday' together.

I leapt onto the table and in just two bounds I attacked

the burning white sticks. I knocked them over and this put out the fire. The trouble was, someone had put the sticks deeply into the birthday cake, and I had been forced to jump right onto the cake to put out the fire. Now I was covered with cake.

'Oliver!' shouted Sophia, and Clint and half his friends started crying and pointing their fingers at me. Nicolas's face went bright red. I didn't know what to do. They should have congratulated me for saving the house from burning down, but all they were worried about was me making the cake a little untidy. I liked a little of the creamy topping and ate it to show everyone that it was just fine, but Clint just cried some more. Then the trouble really started.

Echo began barking very loudly and nonstop. He started pushing people out of the room and there was smoke coming from underneath the table. Then Sophia started yelling, 'Everyone out!' There was a wail of crying toddlers rushing away from the smoke and now a few small flames appeared.

Echo kept his head. He made sure that Lydia and Roger were out of the room then found the kitchen fire extinguisher, picked it up in his mouth and dropped it at Sophia's feet. Sophia used it to spray white foam everywhere. The fire was out. Nan came in and opened the windows and the smoke disappeared. In a few minutes everything was cleaned up.

Except for me. I was covered in cake and white foam, and it all felt horrible. No one seemed to think I should be cleaned up first. I wanted Lucy there, but she was still at school. But Nan came into the room, scooped me up and gave me a bath. Lydia and Echo came along too.

Echo explained that the white sticks I had knocked over were called candles and they were deliberately set alight at birthday parties. 'Dangerous, I know, but that's humans for you — they think it looks nice.' Apparently, they get very hot and even though the flames were out when I knocked them over, they were still dangerous. One of the candles had rolled onto a little piece of paper I had just shredded and that started smoking and set alight a bigger piece of paper. It was just as well Echo noticed this first.

After playing in the hunting grounds, all the children's parents arrived to pick them up in their cars and take them home.

Nicolas's mother had her car door open and Jacques came running towards me, barking. What's wrong with that woman? I stood up, arched my back, hissed and swiped him on the nose. Jacques turned tail and I was beginning to feel triumphant, but then he changed his mind. He turned around and charged right at me, teeth bared. I was so surprised that I was frozen stiff. But Echo kindly walked in between us and told Jacques, 'Get back in your car, son.' Jacques didn't argue and I was glad to have such a protector as Echo. From now I am going to be extra nice to guide dogs. They are the best. I made a point of kissing Lydia and Roger goodbye and making as much fuss over them as I could, so hopefully they will come back with Echo.

Echo said a very nice thing when he left: 'Not every cat I see is as polite to me as you have been. I enjoyed your company, young cat, and look forward to seeing you again.' I gave him a lick, but he was by then focused just on his job.

Day 134

Both Richard and Sophia's cars are going to the house in the country and Nan is coming down the next day on her motorbike. It was agreed that I would travel with Nan. There were lots of suitcases for me to jump in and out of to make sure they all worked. It was noisy, with everyone telling everyone else what to do and bring. I went onto Sophia's bed, hoping to have another chance of getting at the goldfish, but went to sleep instead.

Day 135

I had never travelled on a motorbike before until today. Nan strapped the cat carrier to the luggage rack at the back and I had a good view out of the right-hand side. I thought it would be a very noisy ride, but Nan said her Goldwing Motorcycle was one of the quietest motorbikes in the world. It was smooth and fast, too.

Nan liked overtaking every other vehicle on the road and was doing a lot of that until a very noisy car with flashing lights almost forced us to the curb. Then someone who looked like one of the guards at the hospital got out and asked Nan to turn her engine off. She then asked Nan if she knew why she had been stopped. 'I am sorry, officer,' she said, 'I have no idea. Is there a problem?'

'Can I see your licence please?'

'Thank you,' said the officer as Nan handed over a small card. 'It says you were born in ... well that would make you 78 years old?'

'Yes, that's right officer.'

'I've never seen a mature lady with one these before,' said the officer. 'She is a real beauty, isn't she?'

I thought the officer must have been talking about me, so I meowed to let her know that there was no 'she' about me. I also thought Nan might be in trouble so a distraction might be helpful.

The officer walked around and peered through my door.

'What a cute cat. What's her name?'

'He's called Oliver. Take him out if you like, he is very friendly to people he likes, aren't you Oliver?'

'Well, I suppose I should check to make sure he's travelling safely.'

I took the hint from Nan and once the officer opened the door I jumped into her arms, gave her a lick and snuggled up next to her ear and licked that too. She put me down and I brushed myself all around her legs, meowing for the officer to pick me up again and she did, and we petted each other for several minutes.

A mechanical-sounding male voice in the officer's car rattled away, which caused the officer to say, 'Oh, I'm forgetting myself. I'd better get back to work,' and hand me to Nan. I kissed her hand and headbutted it as she put me down.

'I can't possibly book you two now, Madam. Here is your licence back, thanks, but please drive a lot more slowly — the limit is just 60 here. Now be safe,' she said, and she gave me a farewell pat and drove off.

'Good work, Oliver,' said Nan and for at least the next ten minutes she didn't overtake so many cars or other motorbikes.

Day 136

Lucy met me as we arrived at the very big rented holiday house. She showed me the food and litter arrangements, which were just outside her ground-floor room with its own special cat flap. I decided to sleep.

Day 137

There is a window ledge in Lucy's room, and I was able to sit on it all day, taking careful note of where the birds live and where the mice might be hiding.

Day 138

Explored Lucy's room today. There is an enormous cupboard full of old clothes that I put on the floor to make both the floor and the cupboard more comfortable, and went back to sleep.

Day 139

Just outside my room there are some steps leading to a big open grassy area. I have noticed that I could hide on one side of them and nothing would see me coming before I ambushed it, either on the grass or walking up and down the stairway.

Day 140

It rained all day so I wasn't able to ambush anything. Lucy took me down on her neck to have lunch with everyone. The whole family was there. But Lucy told me that Henry was coming for a visit in a couple of days. She wouldn't have known about him answering her phone and trying to get me stranded in the hospital. But I certainly did.

Day 141

We all had breakfast together outside. Richard, Sophia and Lucy moved the big table down the stairs to the big grassy area. Bubs was free to roam as much as she could. Clint wanted to play ball with me, but now he kicks too hard so I have to dodge when he uses me as a target to practise on. I don't like that very much, but at least I know he has no chance of hitting me.

I practised my ambush techniques on everyone as they went up the stairs back into the house and they seemed to work. I am pleased to have an excellent hiding place. Especially as Henry is coming tomorrow and I will have to deal with him.

Day 142

Today I explored the ground floor of the house. There are no mice or rats. There are seven good sleeping places and three superb high spots for me to base myself on. There is only one cat flap but three outside doors. A dog could come in through the back door of the house unseen, but the two front doors and my own entrance are in full view of everyone. Just to make sure that the back door was secure, I knocked down a nearby stack of brooms and a box of old boots and the door is now properly blocked.

Day 143

Henry called to say he would be a few days late. I gave Lucy extra kisses and snuggles to let her know how happy I was about that. But she responded, 'That's okay, Oliver darling, Henry doesn't matter that much really.' I saw that Sophia agreed with that. Sophia and I looked at each other and we both saw an ally.

'Lucy, why don't you also ask your good friend Bella to come?' suggested Sophia. 'She lives very near here and she could bring Bear too, if that's all right with you, Oliver?' Tail and I showed our happy agreement. Sophia must have a plan and we are happy to help.

Day 144

I explored the top floor of the house today and made sure to check out the room Henry might be sleeping in, which is at the very far end of the house – as far from Lucy and me as possible. Sophia was making up a small bed for him there and we had a lovely chat. She admitted that she was worried about Henry. Some things at home had gone missing around the time he was there. They might just have got lost or taken by the cat-sitter, but she wasn't sure, and anyway she just didn't like Henry.

I clawed at Henry's pillow a couple of times to let Sophia know that I understood and would be on watch. She laughed and said that I was a smart cat.

Day 145

That very strange extra-large table with a chair next to it is actually called a piano. Lucy lifted its lid and showed me how it works. At first, I was so frightened that I went inside it to hide. But very soon I was able to walk up and down the keys and make my own music.

Day 146

Bella and Bear came first. They only live a few minutes' cycle ride away and Bear is happy running along ahead of Bella's bike. Bella and Lucy really like each other, and they spent hours looking at their own and each other's phones together. Then Lucy showed Bella some of her new books and they got into a really long conversation and didn't seem to mind at all when Henry rang to say he would be another two days late.

Day 147

Richard calls being here a summer holiday. I hope we have more of them. Everyone has much more time for me and everyone else. No one is allowed to wear their watch at this house, and Lucy and Bella have promised to stop using their phones.

It's lovely having Bear here. He is twice the size he used to be and even stronger. We remembered a lot about each other, and I heard all about his adventures scaring delivery men. He came to my door early this morning. He told me that Bella was still asleep but he wanted to play and he hoped that I did. Bear had a brand-new collar and said that he didn't mind being on a leash and that I really should try it. We explored all the outside area and later I was the referee while Bear and Bella played football against Lucy and Clint. Bella shared her lunch with me, and after showing Bear the ambush spot, I decided that the day couldn't get any better and went off to sleep.

Day 148

Henry arrived this morning. Lucy, Bella and Bear were all here but everyone else had gone to 'the beach'. Bear told me that 'the beach is about as wet as you can get' so I certainly wouldn't like it. While the three humans talked I carefully showed Bear the whole house, including the sleeping spots, and we decided to test one out together.

Everyone had lunch outside today but I noticed that Henry had quietly left the table and disappeared. I signalled to Bear and we went to hunt for him. I brushed past Sophia's legs to quietly alert her, and I saw that she and Richard exchanged glances.

Bear and I walked outside around the house and saw that Henry was inside. We heard him walk upstairs. We needed to be extra quiet, so I asked Bear to lie in wait at the ambush spot, ready for action. He agreed and settled into place, hidden from everyone. He is a smart dog, Bear, and a good friend too.

I crept into the house as quiet as only a stealthy cat can be. I padded upstairs, avoiding all the creaky bits and staying in the shadows. Henry was moving quietly too, which made me more suspicious as he is normally clumsy and noisy. He was not in his room but I saw his packed bag in the hallway, which seemed much fatter than when I'd

inspected it after he arrived. I undid its zip with my mouth and was about to look inside when I heard him go into Sophia and Richard's room. I crept along the corridor and was so shocked to see Henry put Richard's watch into his pocket that I yowled out load. It was the biggest yowl I had ever done. I was furious. But not as furious as Henry.

I have seen Clint have plenty of tantrums but a teenage boy's is a very ugly sight. Far uglier and scarier than Jacques when he was attacking me. Henry stomped after me downstairs, picking up his bag on the way. I turned around and spat at him. He chased me into Lucy's room and kept coming so I spat at him again then escaped and zoomed down the stairs towards the lunch table.

Bear lunged out of his hiding spot at the perfect moment and Henry went flying through the air, as did all the contents of his bag, which included Richard's bottles and Nan's motorcycle gloves.

Lucy screamed but everyone else went quiet. Richard saw what had come out of the bag and sat on Henry until the police came. The police found Richard's watch and took Henry away. Lucy was very upset, so I comforted her until Sophia picked me up and grabbed Bear and said, 'It's fresh steak and fish for you boys today,' and we went into the kitchen.

Day 149

The day was spent kissing, comforting and petting Lucy.
Other than Bear, Richard and me, she now hates all males.
I hope that doesn't include Echo.

Day 150

Lucy now hates Richard after he suggested that she 'get up
and get over it'.

Day 151

Lucy got up and got over it and said that tomorrow, Bella,
Bear and the two of us are going on a long bicycle ride into
the countryside.

Day 152

We left after breakfast, with Lucy all covered up against
the sun. She put a little coat and a hat on me. It matched my
collar, so I didn't mind too much.

Normally, I don't like humans dressing me up as if
I'm a toy. I allow Bubs to do this as she doesn't know any

better, and Sophia or Nan always distract her before she goes too far. But today it was hot and even Bear had a sun screening coat on. I started running along behind Bella and Lucy but I really couldn't keep up so got into the basket on Lucy's bicycle. Bear is very strong and kept going for hours. I encouraged him from my basket. There is a big basket at the back of Bella's bicycle which can just fit Bear. But he is still growing very quickly so it won't be much use very soon.

We went out in the wild areas and there were hardly any cars, and it was so hot that even the birds were quiet. We stopped to say hello to a horse and its rider. The horse asked me to make sure Bear stayed still as 'there's been trouble with dogs around here'.

The horse then started talking at length.

'You are a cat aren't you, but you're not like the ones around here. There's just a few of them. Proper wild, they are, and I wouldn't be believing any of their stories if they catch up with you. They just talk and talk, and the racket will make your tail stand upright, it will. No, you are house cat indeed, all clean and quiet, like. Mind, though, I haven't seen one of you lot with a hat on before, or riding a bicycle, come to that. Bit irregular if you ask me.'

The rider told Lucy there was a path across the fields that we could cycle on which would take us into the big woods. We thanked him and found the path, and in a few moments we were in very old woodland. It took me a while to adjust to the light, the many new smells and the different sounds. Although the sun was almost at its height, the air in the woodlands still seemed like it was early morning. We sat down for lunch. I shared Bella's sandwiches and Bear quickly shared everything, and then I heard a strange noise.

The noise repeated itself, magnified and spread in a wave of sound that bounced off the trees. I was too fascinated to be scared. Bear wasn't interested and Lucy said they were crickets. I found one. It was a big, long insect folded tightly together and attached to a lower part of a tree trunk. I walked over to watch it rub its legs together to make a very loud 'click click' sound. Sometimes when it did that, the wave of sound erupted and crashed against the woodland. All the crickets were making the same sound at the same time. It was thrilling and deafening, even more so than the rock music Nan plays.

Somehow, though, the crickets' sound seemed to belong where it was and that was very peaceful, so we all settled for a little snooze. Some little white-winged insects came to say hello and I was so relaxed that I didn't even dab at them. One stopped on my nose for a second or two and it was so peaceful that I was happy to provide a temporary resting place. A dragonfly hovered above us and was joined by another and together they spiralled and spun in an ever-shrinking circle. I fell asleep mesmerized by their unhurried certainty.

We all woke up at the same time. The air had changed. Now it felt heavy and warm, and all was quiet. Instead of the morning freshness, the air was heavy with the sweet sticky smell of lime and cypress trees.

We didn't stay long in the woods, but it made a big impression upon me. There is much in this world that is intriguing, scary and mysterious that I do not understand. There is so much to do and find out, but I think I just prefer being with Lucy.

Day 153

I woke up in Lucy's bed this morning. It's such a comfortable place that I decided to stay there all day. All night too, if I am lucky. Lucy doesn't seem to mind; she is not seeing Bella today and she said that she had to catch up with her own journal writing. I have already done mine, so it is sleep time.

Day 154

Today I had to run. After whizzing through the house and nearly tripping up Nan, who was carrying her morning glass and bottle, I went across the grass into the hunting grounds beyond. I ran around them imagining that Bear and I were in a race and that I was winning. I would win against Bear in a short race, but if it lasted for more than five minutes he would win. I found the thought of losing to a dog, even my good friend Bear, a bit depressing so I went back into the house for some comfort and sat on Sophia's lap while she was watching a film. It was the same film that Richard had on all the time, called *The Godfather II*. Like all cats, I prefer *The Godfather I* as we have a significant role, but there are some ideas in the sequel that intrigue me.

Day 155

The world is full of amazing things and one of them is the human incapacity for staying with decisions. Bear and I decide and we do it. That's all there is to it. I may be a bit uncertain about things but once I have made up my mind I will go ahead. Unless of course I get bored, find something more interesting, or think it might be wet, unbecoming or unsafe. But humans change their minds all the time.

We were all supposed to be going back home today but we are now staying for a whole two weeks more. I am happy about this, especially if they keep their phones and watches off, as they are so much nicer when they do. Also, I will get to see lots more of Bear.

Day 156

Everyone was cross this morning and very quiet. I think it's because someone left too many empty bottles on the kitchen table. It was Richard's birthday and because he is big, he doesn't get to eat cake. Frankly, that's a good thing, as he has become much bigger this holiday. You could hide a whole one of me inside him and nobody would notice. I was glad that he announced, to nobody, that he was taking up jogging tomorrow.

Day 157

This house leaks. There is a bucket in Lucy's room that I haven't yet managed to knock over, but I will. Now there is a little stream coming through the back door. Richard is swearing at it, which I think will help. But I helped more by pushing that box of old boots back in its way. We will know if it worked by the morning.

Day 158

It didn't work and Richard decided to swear even harder. He used a lot of words I have not heard him use before so I think he must have been getting lessons from Nan's bottles. Apparently, it was raining 'cats and dogs' but I didn't see any. But maybe I was dreaming so I went to sleep to check if I was.

Day 159

Everyone had their watches back on today and talked at and tapped on their phones. Pity.

'There is no point in staying here, puss,' said Richard, picking me up. 'The weather is going to get worse and we need to get home before the road gets flooded and we get stuck for weeks.' I made myself scarce as everyone spent the whole day packing for the trip home.

Day 160

We left just as the birds woke up, Richard driving in the front with Lucy and Bubs, who was fast asleep, and me in the back. I pretended to be a toy cat and draped my full length on the ledge of the back windscreen. Then came Sophia and Clint. I think that whizzing blur was Nan on the Goldwing, playing her music ever louder as she accelerated yet more.

There were lots of other cars following us into town and I liked seeing the passengers' faces when I occasionally got up and turned around on the ledge.

Day 161

It is wonderful being back home. I am going to have a day sleeping in all my favourite spots to make sure they are still the same.

Day 162

Two of my sleeping spots felt even better than they did before; will try two more today.

Day 163

Lucy woke me up to say she'd had a telephone call asking if we wanted to come for a sleepover at Bella's at the weekend. Bella's parents would pick us up tomorrow.

I am excited to be going on a sleepover. I have never been to one before. Whenever Clint's friends have a sleepover there is a lot of cake, jelly, shouting and talking. I hope this is a bit quieter.

Day 164

Bella's parents have got the biggest vehicle ever, and as soon as they had parked outside, Bear leapt out and showed me around. Inside the vehicle was like a whole house for humans. It has a sofa, which Bear told me becomes a bed, a television (humans don't seem to manage without them), a whole kitchen with a promising-smelling fridge, a kind of bathroom and another bedroom in the roof. Wow. I hope we are going to sleepover in this.

Bear showed me his travelling kennel, which fitted in the roof during the day and which he slept in outside at night.

Bella's mother is called Marion. She is very calm and in charge, and she does the driving. Bella's dad is called Mike. He never stopped talking and pointing at things he found

interesting as we were driving. I don't know who he was talking to, though; it couldn't have been Bear or me, and Lucy and Bella were busy sending each other messages.

Day 165

We drove to a lake today and parked up for the night and I finally learnt what Mike was for.

Mike took out some long poles with a lot of thin string attached to them and a pretty, shiny metal thing (which I later learnt was called a lure) tied to the front of the string. I moved forward to have a good look but Bear stopped me.

'Nasty metal hooks and wire to get tripped up in there, and be careful when there is a fish on the end as the hook will still be there.'

A fish!

Mike held onto the pole and threw the lure as far into the lake as he could, and then using a little handle on the end of the pole he brought the lure back in. It looked interesting but I couldn't see what it had to do with fish. After his third throw and reel-in routine, Bear and I lost interest and chased each other around the motor home. But then

Marion shouted 'Yippee!' and there was already a small fish on the ground. Mike took out the lure and offered it to me. I checked with Bear. 'Can't say I like the stuff — I'm a meat and biscuits only dog. Will eat fish If I have to but only when it's cooked.'

Mike caught enough fish to make me his number one admirer for the day and cooked it all up for everyone on an open fire by the lake. That was a good night, but I am going to try fishing myself tomorrow.

Day 166

I slept on top of Bear in his kennel while he kept guard of the motor home. We were up before the humans, and we crept down to the water's edge to look for my breakfast. They had left the van's door ajar, so I checked on Lucy first and she was fine. I gave her a kiss but landed on Mike's toes on my way out and he said something about dangerous tigers being on the loose.

This tiger and Bear saw a lot of fish. Bear told me that it is called a shoal of fish and it was right on the water's edge. Bear jumped in with a big splash and a bark, landing in the middle of the shoal. The fish scattered but (faster than a normal tiger) I leapt in and scooped one up with both front paws. It was cold, wet and wriggly, and it slithered, in a very unsporting way, out of my grasp and swam away to join its friends.

A very big fish arrived and though it kept a little way from the water's edge I was scared. The big fish was at least twice the size of a rabbit. It had cold eyes and a big jaw.

Bear couldn't care less and jumped in the water and swam after it, but it disappeared. Bear is so brave. Such a good friend to have.

Bear and I were telling each other how brave we were when a small fish floated to the surface. Bear might have stunned it when he first jumped in the lake. Bear swam out and pushed it to the shore. I caught it and we agreed that I should give it as a present to Marion for bringing us here.

Marion was still asleep so I dropped the fish in the water glass right next to her bed so she would find it easily. She was obviously very happy about it as I heard her shouting a lot.

Day 167

Marion, Mike and Bella have taken to calling me Fish Tiger, which I like. But this afternoon on the drive back home Lucy cuddled me and said I will always be her Oliver, which made me very happy.

Day 168

I am rather missing Bear now that we have come home, and I forgot to ask for his help with those rabbits. I spent the morning thinking about my strategy for dealing with them. It's going to be difficult.

By the afternoon I still hadn't reached any conclusions as to what to do with the rabbits. But I have a few ideas. First, I zoomed around the hunting grounds to see if they were still there. They were and they haven't stopped breeding and have made even more holes. They are

completely out of order, showing no respect for my family. Tomorrow I will set my trap.

Day 169

On the other side of our property is a market garden. They grow things that rabbits are supposed to eat: cabbages, lettuces, carrots and other disgusting things. Whoever is in charge there will care a lot about rabbits. I have patrolled their hedges and fences and there is no way through. But if I can find a way to let the rabbits in, seeing their lettuces being eaten might make the garden's owner want to work with me to deal with them.

Day 170

Today I asked the rabbits nicely to move out. They charged at me and there were too many of them even for Fish Tiger, so I had to escape. Will put my plan into action soon. I wish Bear was here.

Day 171

Rabbits sleep at night. But Fish Tigers don't have to. I padded past their burrows, across the bridge into the woods and onto the neighbours' fence line and jumped over. Patrolling from their side showed me the one weakness. They had put all their old leaves and dead branches in a big rotting pile against the fence and it looked like the fence was slowly collapsing against the age and weight of it all. I needed to encourage that process and draw the rabbits' attention to their lettuce opportunity.

Day 172

Had to sleep, to work on the remaining issues. The fence was far stronger than I was and even if I managed to create a gap how would I get the rabbits to make use of it? Rabbits are both obstinate and stupid. I then remembered that Bear and Bella are coming back tomorrow, and I went very happily to sleep on it.

Day 173

Bear was keen to help and charged straightaway at the fence. It didn't take him long to create a hole even the fattest rabbit could crawl through. We then made a path to the lettuce patch that even the stupidest bunny couldn't miss.

Day 174

We checked first thing, but it was obvious the rabbits had not found the path. So Bear and I went to visit them and got them to promise not to ever use the path, and we made it clear that I would be very cross if they did. It was my private path, not to be used by rabbits, even if there were plenty of lettuces on the other side. Bear growled a bit and they promised and we went home.

Day 175

First thing this morning there were two big snarling dogs and a man dressed like a scarecrow banging on our door.

Nan opened the door and the scarecrow held on tightly to his dogs, who tried to rush at me.

'Take those away and come back without them,' said Nan. 'I'm not talking to you with those dogs.' And she closed the door. She was so brave. I rubbed against her legs and she picked me up, saying, 'That just won't do, will it, Oliver?' and I gave her a lick.

They are Rottweilers, 'nasty dogs that would eat you as soon as look at you,' said Bear, who added, 'I'm not even sure I would win a fight against two of them.'

Ten minutes later the scarecrow came back. He looked calmer and there was a lady with him, brandishing two half-eaten lettuces at Richard, who'd opened the door this time. 'And you can take those away too,' said Nan of the lettuces. She'd already told Richard what had previously happened.

Richard explained that we didn't keep any rabbits, but yes there were many on our property. But if they would care to buy them from him he wouldn't have a problem.

Day 176

All the rabbits had already gone today and there was a large pile of fresh vegetables on the kitchen table. Bear and I are proud of what we have achieved here. The enemy has been vanquished and the family enriched. It's time Bear and I thought about extending our influence.

Day 177

This morning Lucy said that the nice lady from the hospital had called and explained that their therapy cat was having a week off and would it be all right if I filled in for a while? Any times would suit. Lucy asked if Bear could come as well, and she thought that was a good idea as they needed new dogs to train. So tomorrow we are therapy cat and dog.

Day 178

They sent a van to pick us up this morning and Bear and I were kitted out in special hospital coats. The officer dog recognized me as I got out the van.

'Nice to see you again sir, and with your assistant too — very sensible choice of dog, if you don't mind me saying so. Have an efficient, orderly day and let me know If I can be of assistance.' We thanked him and said that we were there to help him too, and then went upstairs and reported for duty.

Day 179

It has taken a while for me to get used to wearing a leash, but Lucy persisted, and it does carry the advantage of lots of people wanting to say hello whenever we go out walking. I wore one at the hospital, where Bear and I worked again today. Bear was always comfortable with his leash, but today he went off for 'special training' somewhere in the hospital and the nice lady, Whitney, was going to be my handler today. Lucy was feeling unwell.

Being a therapy cat is pretty similar to my ordinary life. I get moved around on a leash and chat with people. I think it must get boring being in a hospital bed all day, so a bit of company cannot be a bad thing.

Whitney really believes that dogs and cats make the best companions, and I heard a story about her. A few weeks ago, a man came into the hospital for a stay of several months. He was going to be away from home for so long that he was forced to put his beloved cat into a shelter. Whitney found this out, went to the shelter and adopted the cat. She brings him to visit every day. As soon as the man is out of hospital, she will return the cat to him.

Whitney dropped a little white ping pong ball onto the floor of one of the wards and I chased after it. It went

everywhere, under people's beds and near the doctor's feet. I managed to swipe it so hard that it took off and landed on a man being pushed in a wheelchair. I jumped aboard, gave the man a kiss and swiped the ball onto a nearby bed. The gentleman in that bed hit it back with his book and I swiped it onto the opposite bed. He moved it to the bed next to him and then it came back to me, and this went on right through the ward. The ping pong ball was going everywhere, and all the men were joining in. But then Whitney picked me up, saying, 'You are supposed to be peaceful and restful, little puss, not causing riots.' But she was laughing as she said it, as were the men.

Whitney took me into a smaller ward and gently put me on a bed. The face of the very old lady in the bed looked as thin as tissue paper and her hands, though gentle, reminded me of a large bird.

'Hello Mary,' said Whitney. 'This is Oliver, who has come to say hello.'

'Oh, a cat, how nice,' Mary said, stroking me very cautiously, and I saw that her eyes were moist.

'You are a big kitten really aren't you, dear?'

I have never seen anyone quite as old as that lady. Everything about her seemed still and quiet, as if time had stopped around her and her frail presence was hovering at its edge. But I wanted to know about her in the here and now, so I kissed her fingers and then snuggled right up next to her on her pillow so she could settle down and we could look into each other's eyes. I purred and made my 'ooff ooff' noises, which are normally reserved for my favourite foods, and Mary gave me the best smile ever. She playfully and cautiously moved her hand towards me across the bed and I gently swatted it with my paw. We repeated this for a while but then I think I must have gone to sleep. I woke up as she moved right up in the bed.

'Ooh, Oliver, you are a real tonic and that's no mistake,' she said, and she gave me a kiss and settled back down to sleep. This time I could hear her breathing, which became smoother and deeper. Cats know that peace and comfort are not always the same thing but Mary seemed to have united the two.

Day 180

Lucy and I went back to the hospital and found Mary, who was awake this time and very pleased to see us, and I snuggled right up to her and got another of her dazzling smiles. I found a vase of flowers in the hallway outside and killed a bright red one and dropped it on her lap.

Later, Whitney said that we had done Mary a lot of good and could come back any time we liked. But she added that she was going to take on a more mature cat that had fewer commitments than me so could reliably turn up every day. I think I got fired – but I don't mind as the food was rubbish anyway. I would like to go and see Mary again though.

Day 181

Nan was asleep, it was just midday, and Richard and Lucy had decided to drive to town to buy some jogging gear. Sophia, Clint, Bubs and I were playing in the big lounge room and Richard asked if we wanted to come but Sophia said, 'We're fine thanks.' But I slipped quietly into Lucy's big bag and off we went.

'Oh, Dad, look who's here,' Lucy said as I jumped out of the bag onto her lap just as Richard was parking outside Galactic Sports.

'Well, he'd better stay in the car,' said Richard, stroking my head to make me feel better about it. They said they wouldn't be long, so I stretched out on the back windscreen ledge and went to sleep.

But I was woken up very quickly. The car was moving but there was no one driving it. It was being pulled out of the parking space by a large truck with flashing yellow lights. The truck driver obviously hadn't seen me, so I made myself as big and noisy as possible, but he took no notice. Then something made him stop and he climbed out of the truck and came around the back of the car to have a look.

'You can't take that car away. There's a cat in it,' said a tall lady who was walking past.

'I've got to; it's parked illegally and cat or no cat this car is going to be towed away,' replied the truck driver.

'You can't do that! That's cruelty to animals that is. They will have you up on a charge.'

I tried to make myself look as cute and stressed as possible. This was a difficult combination that had me chasing my tail around the car and popping up at each window in turn.

'Ah, nonsense! Stupid animal is going down to the pound with the car,' the driver said, and he turned back towards his truck.

Just then, though, there were more flashing lights — this time red — and a police car stopped and the officer got out to see what was going on. At the same time, Richard and Lucy came running along the street. It turns out they weren't allowed to leave the car parked there for more than a couple of minutes, but the police officer said it wasn't well signed and the tow truck driver should release the car. He did, and when Richard opened the doors I jumped out and into the policeman's arms and gave him a kiss and found the tall lady and thanked her too. While no one was looking I left my mark on the tow truck and the driver's lunch box.

Day 182

Richard is convinced that wearing the sports clothes he bought yesterday will make him lose weight. He put them on and looked very smart, then sat down to watch television. I needed a lap for the day, so it suited me fine and he didn't protest very much.

Day 183

Sophia picked me up and put me in front of a plant she had recently planted in the hunting grounds. She said it was called catnip. It looks like some of the plants she picks to flavour food, but it offers an entirely different experience. It smelt and tasted so good that I think I felt like Nan does after her morning bottle. I put as much as I could in my mouth and thoroughly washed myself with it, so I am carrying its deliriously delicious smell with me.

I think I understand Nan a bit more now. Sophia was very lovely to introduce me to this plant, as it has changed my life. It is quite simply the very best thing there ever was after Lucy.

Day 184

I had a dream last night where Bear drove a tow truck bringing a whole forest of catnip bushes, and Echo was in front of him directing the traffic.

Day 185

There were big changes at home today. Some time ago Richard put what looked like a big dead tree near Lucy's room. I have been climbing on it, pouncing on people's feet from it, scratching myself all over it and have made it a critical centre of operations.

I came back inside from the hunting grounds today and it had gone. I looked throughout the house for it and couldn't find it anywhere.

Day 186

Last night I was so furious about the large dead tree being moved that I jumped on Richard's bed in the middle of the night to find out what was happening. But he just patted me, and we both went to sleep. So this morning (after Sophia threw me out of their room), I went into the hunting grounds feeling quite out of sorts. Lucy has gone away for a couple of weeks with Nan on the back of her motorbike. Richard and Sophia have hidden my main base of operations and thrown me out of their bedroom. Bubs keeps trying to dress me up like one of their dolls and every time Clint sees me, he kicks a large ball at me. This place isn't as nice as it was, and I am very worried.

Day 187

I haven't had fish for weeks now. With Lucy and Nan away, I just get fed from tins and packets. This really isn't good enough. I am going to have to think about my future.

Day 188

Thought about my future all day and it was too tiring. Practised vertical take-off jumps; they could become very useful.

Day 189

I decided to see if things improved today and not change anything. The food was still boring though, and Richard and Sophia don't seem to even like each other anymore. Sophia has also taken to shouting at Clint which makes Bubs cry. I try to distract her and that sometimes works, particularly when I trip Clint up.

Day 190

At least they left the door to Lucy's room open so I could sleep there. But it doesn't smell quite the same as they have taken away all those interesting meal plates, cups and glasses.

Tomorrow I will come up with a plan. I need to make sure that my family stays safe, but as I am no longer treated properly, I might as well see if there are other places I can live. Just for a while, until Lucy comes back. I would like to see Bear, but he really is a long way away and that's a bit scary. I could go back to the hospital; I am sure Whitney and Mary would like to see me and the officer guard dog too, but the food really isn't any good there.

We were supposed to have gone back to the country place, but they all changed their minds again. I was disappointed about not seeing Bear and meeting the cats the horse was talking about — those cats sounded interesting. I have heard about wild cats before but have been warned that some of them can be very fierce indeed. One of the cats around here, Zinger, talks about the incredibly long, fine hair of the wild grey-haired breed. I should go and find Zinger; he has lots of other interesting stories about cats. One of Zinger's stories is horrifying — apparently some people, especially the Spanish, like wearing our skins.

This afternoon Sophia and Richard were shouting at each other and this time it went on longer than it normally does and seemed a whole lot louder. Then a door got slammed, and then another. And did I hear a glass breaking?

I am feeling very alone and frightened by all this. I will go and see Zinger tomorrow.

Day 191

Zinger told me lots of interesting stories about brave and heroic cats. He also told me how cats used to have god-like status in somewhere called Egypt because they killed snakes. Well, I have killed a snake so I don't see why I should stay somewhere that I am not fed properly and have important parts of my territory removed, let alone be somewhere where a little boy kicks big balls hard and straight at me and the adults throw things at each other.

I am going to go off on a big adventure where I can be treated how Egyptian cats were. Lucy used to do that, I think, but even her smell is beginning to fade.

I waited by the door for the rest of the day for Lucy and Nan to come back, but they are still away.

Day 192

This is going to be my last night here for some time. Lucy is still not back, the food still comes out of a tin, Sophia just hisses at Richard and ignores me. Richard spends his time in the garage workshop, and he is so noisy that I cannot even sit on my usual roof spot.

Bubs caught me by surprise today when I was napping and pulled Tail quite hard. I yelped and swiped at her, but all Sophia did was pick up Bubs and ignore me. Yes, I am going.

Day 193

It was raining today so I stayed home where at least I get fed and it's dry.

Day 194

Still raining so stayed on Lucy's bed. Still no fish.

Day 195

It stopped raining in the night and very quickly the moon appeared. It was full and I could hear other cats, some familiar, some unknown, singing, shouting and talking near my hunting grounds. I heard Lolly and Nameless's voices and prowled out to join them.

'You are not allowed here, little house puss,' said an enormous old black cat with tattered ears and just a few whiskers. 'This moon party is for club members only. Now clear off or I will swipe you away.'

'I am no house cat — I am snake killer,' I said, and at that I pulled myself up to full height and executed such a good vertical take-off that the black cat thought I would land on her. She ran off with a yelp. Then other cats started running around in a big circle and leaping and yodelling.

But the clouds came back, and the moon was hidden for the night, and everything became still.

'Well blow me, that was a leap and a half, wasn't it now?' said Nameless. 'That's just gone and made you a member of the club, hasn't it, Oliver?'

It was good to see Nameless, with Lolly right beside him. They both looked larger and sleeker than before, and Nameless explained that there were excellent vermin in or near the hardware store and that he and Lolly seemed set for life.

'No big birds you see; too many low buildings, poles and lights there, isn't there? Been nothing stopping the vermin for years, has there? It's all there you know: rats, mice, shrews, voles, even some feral gerbils and them little pig things and rabbits and all. Told you you should have got into vermin, didn't I? That's the business, young Oliver, that's where the future is, vermin, isn't that right? Know what I mean? Vermin, that's the cat's business, isn't it?'

Before he could carry on further, Lolly asked how my life was and I explained it all.

'Well, an adventure you must have,' said Lolly, 'and you will only regret it if you don't. And the things you will see, learn, sniff, eat and rub against will make you a smarter cat. Cats don't ever regret things. That doesn't mean we don't get sad from time to time but we regret nothing ever.'

I bid them both a happy good night and went back home to bed. It was a bit cold and wet outside and an adventurous cat needs his sleep.

Day 196

Today I decided I needed more sleep so put up with more tinned food, more banging in the garage, and more of Sophia and Richard noisily ignoring each other, and slept most of the day.

Day 197

Everyone has left the house and it's just me inside. Well, I won't be here when they get back. Serves them right for abandoning me. But they have left me enough food for three days, so I don't think that I will rip anything up in protest.

Day 198

I sat by the front gate this morning waiting for Lucy as usual, and the tall lady who'd helped me out with the tow truck man walked by. I was very pleased to see her, and I am sure that she recognized me. We had quite a long chat and she gave me a good lot of attention. She even gently tickled my ears, which shows that she understands cats, and I gave her some nice kisses.

Day 199

The tall lady came back this evening and she asked me where all my family was. I looked sad and made little kitten meow sounds. She said that, if I wanted, I could come and stay with her until they came back. She lived alone and said that she only ate fish but would be happy to share that. It was quiet tonight, so I followed her home and I let her carry me through the busy roads. I decided that I was more comfortable in her bag than walking myself, and soon enough she let me into her house.

There was a cat flap which the lady opened.

'It's not been used for years,' she explained. 'There used to be a cat that lived here with me, but she died, and I loved her so much I haven't had the heart to invite another cat home. She was nineteen years old, too.'

Soon there were proper cat bowls with fish and water, a freshly cleaned litter box and she showed me somewhere safe and warm to sleep on the sofa. But I've decided to sleep on the nice lady's bed tonight.

Day 200

It was fish for breakfast, and then the nice lady, whose name I discovered is Margaret, said that she had to go out to work today, but I was welcome to come and go as I pleased. I was a bit scared being in the house without Margaret, so I stayed in her bedroom most of the day.

When Margaret came home, I became a brave cat and explored the house. Margaret's home is smaller than my family's but there are enough places to hide and though there are not any goldfish inside, I think I saw something move in the pond in the hunting grounds. Something to investigate further.

Day 201

I spent the day by the pond trying not to think about Lucy. I was wondering why she had abandoned me and thought that something terrible must have happened to her. But then I clearly saw a golden fish move in the pond. Then another and then another and another. There were at least four or five fish in there and I was sure Margaret wouldn't miss one. Or two. But how to catch them?

After I had taught Margaret how to play with some ping pong balls, which I'd found getting dusty on a shelf, she went to bed, and I started to think about fishing techniques and went outside to look at them. It was a full moon, but the

fish were very still, all huddled together next to each other at the bottom of the pond.

The pond is far too deep for me to wade in, and I don't like the idea of diving in to catch them. I am going to have to wait till they come to the surface, then scoop them up with my paws.

Day 202

This afternoon I was busy watching the fish when Margaret came outside and bounced a ping pong ball off a nearby tree and it tried to escape into the hedge. I caught it and bashed it away, but the cheeky thing bounced off the wall and hit me on the nose. That wasn't playing fair. I jumped up and pounced on it, but it slipped out and landed in the pond. I was, of course, about to go straight in after it, but I saw there was another ping pong ball lurking in wait for me, so I knocked it down the path and it sneaked through the front gate and onto the footpath. I jumped over the gate to get it ... and there was Lucy!

I was so surprised that I forgot to show her how angry I was for deserting me for so long. Seeing Lucy was like catnip, long and short sleeps, fresh fish, kisses, ear stroking and full cuddles and more fresh fish all rolled into one perfect sensation. After I had finished rolling on the ground, Lucy picked me up and told me that Margaret had phoned her to say that I was safe where I was and to pick me up whenever suited.

Margaret is a very lovely woman and before Lucy and I left for our house I rescued one of her fish out of that nasty overcrowded pond and put it on her back doorstep as a thank you gift. I hope she found it.

Lucy took me back home in her bicycle's basket and I took very careful note of the route so I could be sure to find it on my own next time. I would like to see the fish soon. Margaret too.

Day 203

This morning was payback time. I sat in the middle of the kitchen and ignored everyone all day. This afternoon I slept in front of the bathroom door. This evening I sat on the TV remote control.

Day 204

Richard and Sophia are being nicer. They even pat each other occasionally, and Richard certainly spent more time with Bubs and Clint today. However, the food is still coming out of tins and Richard is still making a horrible noise in the garage and my territory has not been put back. Also, now that she keeps wanting to pull my tail, I am not sure how cute Bubs is.

Day 205

There was a rabbit back in the hunting grounds today. This could be a problem; they are far too cheeky and breed in ridiculous numbers very quickly. Rabbits are also stupid, destructive and messy. But they are fun to chase, and stalking them is an interesting sport. This one was a solitary young male, and he didn't seem very happy to see me. I chased him out of the hunting grounds but he went the wrong way — not towards the market garden as I intended but right into Sophia's herb patch. I like that part of the hunting grounds, as many of the herbs are good to have a little nibble on now and again — and of course my special catnip is there and that, most definitely, is not for rabbits.

I chased the rabbit and he ran into the road without looking where he was going. There were some horrible noises and suddenly there were several angry people jumping out of their cars, pointing their fingers and shouting at each other. Humans can either be very scary or very ridiculous when they are angry. One driver had stopped to avoid hitting the rabbit. But the person behind him drove into the back of his car and the person behind did the same thing.

Exactly the same thing happened on the other side of the road and the people over there were also outside their cars shouting at each other. Then the people behind them shouted and so it went on.

I sat up on our wall and watched the proceedings. Richard stopped his banging and came and joined me. A police officer on a motorbike drove into the area and put his pretty flashing lights on and another one did the same on the other side of the road. But they didn't do anything else, as they were soon surrounded by people trying to shout louder than each other.

Then, driving half on the pavement and half on the

road, a tow truck came along, and it was being driven by the same nasty man who had tried to steal our car. He was clearly going to steal as many of these poor people's cars as possible. I was going to have to stop him.

He walked towards one of the police officers just as another motorcycle police officer parked behind him. I leapt through the window onto the driver's seat of the tow truck to see what I could do and pushed and pressed every lever that I could and then jumped out quickly.

Before I had even returned to my wall there was an enormous set of crashes and bangs. The tow truck had gone as mad as the driver was about to. First, it sent out a metal bar from its very back to knock over the police officer's motorbike. The driver came rushing back, waving his fists at either the officer or the truck. He hit the officer. The truck then sent another big metal bar right up high and mangled a streetlight. The driver raised his hands to the air either in shock or to hit the other two police officers who were there. He hit both. Then the truck lifted the police bike and attached it to the remains of the light. The truck then sent an arm out either side of its front, gripped the road and lifted itself up but then came down with a big bang, smashing the pavement.

I was amazed at how careless and aggressive this driver had been, and all three police officers agreed. They were so angry that two of them sat on him and ordered another tow truck to take away the remains of his truck. Then a police car with three more officers came to take the driver away while he yelled that he was 'not a terrorist'. Then other tow trucks came to remove the cars that wouldn't start. Yet another truck took the lamppost away, another one took the remains of the motorbike, and another truck came with workers and a machine to fix up the pavement.

Rabbits cause such a lot of trouble, and I am going to have to chase them all away whenever I see them.

Day 206

Lucy told me that Richard and I were on the television news. He looked like the nice, calm cardigan-wearing man he is, and of course I looked like my cute kitten self. I just hope that the tow truck driver didn't see it and recognize me from the previous time.

Day 207

I spent the morning chasing Lucy's toes with a brand-new strategy. First, while she was asleep with her slippers on, I quietly and peacefully dismantled one of the slippers and then pounced. Lucy then came rushing at me, waving the remains of her slipper. I do like how Lucy gets into the spirit of things. I was ready to go in for the killer toe bite when Lucy shouted, 'Stop, Oliver!' extra loudly. I, of course, stopped right away, as I am a very well-behaved cat. Lucy seemed quite pleased that I had stopped, and she gave me a hug.

I thought that Lucy might have become too old to play with her toes, but I haven't, so I went in search of Clint. He has got fat toes and they are easy to pounce on. But Nan picked me up mid-pounce and successfully distracted me by taking me into the kitchen. No fish, though.

Day 208

Richard left the garage door open today while he was banging away, and I summoned up the courage to block out the sound and investigate what he was doing. But as soon as I walked in, he walked out and closed the door and stomped off. I meowed and meowed, but no one heard me and I had to spend all afternoon on my own locked in the garage.

Day 209

I decided that Richard owed me extra attention today because of yesterday's unacceptable imprisonment. I climbed onto his neck at breakfast time, shared his toast and then went back to sleep upon him. I woke up as Richard walked back into the garage, and there I saw what he had been bashing away at. Richard has rebuilt my indoor territory base!

What was suitable for an energetic little kitten has now been made appropriate for a Fish Tiger, tow truck slayer, moon club member, rabbit-terrorizing puss like me. It is many times the size it was. Mind you, so am I, so that's only right. There are new up bits, down bits, across bits, things to slide on and hide in, and lots of places at lots of levels to jump from.

Sophia, Lucy and Nan joined us, and Bubs and Clint came along too, and Richard carefully dismantled my territory into a few parts and put them in the house where my territory used to be.

Richard spent the rest of the day banging and swearing as normal, putting the parts back together. But at least now I could see the point of the noise. Finally, when they had their bottles open in the evening, Lucy carried me upstairs to the grand opening. She put me on the very top part where she held out a ribbon covered with catnip, and I was very happy using my Fish Tiger lethal teeth to cut it. I spent the rest of the night exploring this great space. I have no doubt that using it will improve my speed and sharpen my fighting and hunting skills. I am going to be ready for serious action tomorrow.

Day 210

I had such a good time last night that I slept all day today.

Day 211

I think my family is lovely. How could I ever have doubted them? I gave everyone (even Bubs) extra kisses today. There was fish for breakfast.

Day 212

Lucy came back with some books she borrowed from a library and attempted to get me interested in them. I like books, as whenever they are opened, people become quieter, gentler and calmer. Everyone here except Clint and Bubs reads quite a bit, and Nan and Richard read aloud to them, too. I enjoy those times as everyone involved, including me, follows the story.

Today, though, the books were supposed to be for me. First, there was a book of poetry for cats and Lucy read some of the poems aloud. I enjoyed one about a fat red cat who got stuck in his cat flap. There was a funny poem about a Persian cat who hid a tribe of mice in the house owner's hat, and another one about a cat who just lived in order to nap. Now that sounds like a perfect life.

Day 213

Lucy still hasn't stopped with the books. Now she is showing me one on how to teach cats to read; yesterday she tried one on how cats can paint. This is all silly; we don't want books on reading or painting in oils. If we must read (and really we must not, as that's a human's job) we should have practical books on how to train humans better and how to be better at fishing.

While Lucy read mostly to herself today, I had a good, long meditative look at my white socks. I still think that they are extraordinary. I will ask Bear what he thinks.

Day 214

Today involved an epic effort on my part. I manged to drag Flippity Fish on to the top part of my indoor territory. It took a long time as it protested a lot and wiggled and grunted away to all sorts of places. I have decided to drop it on Clint's head the next time he tries to climb up.

Lucy said that she and I had to go and see the vet tomorrow for some routine injections and inspections. I don't like that idea at all. But Lucy was very clear that the appointment had been made and that Richard was going to drive us.

Day 215

I spent the day hiding in next door's big apple tree. I didn't ask to go to the vets, so I ignored everyone when they called out for me.

Humans have a different tone of voice they use for each reason they are calling me. A quick 'puss puss puss' means they are confident I will be there soon as it's dinner time. They are always right about that. Whereas a long 'Oliveeer, Oliveeer, Oliveeer' means they haven't got a clue where I am but think I ought to be home now. I let that one stretch on for a long time as it's about their business, not mine. On the other hand, when Lucy needs my company she calls my name just once and very softly and I come immediately. When Richard or Sophia just shout 'Oliver! Oliver!' I ignore that, as they are likely to be grumpy about something. Nan calls me at times, normally to help her play with the very young ones – 'Oliver darling, Oliver darling' – and it's part of my job to do that, so I normally come right away. Except when I am doing something more interesting or if I am busy in the hunting grounds or about to go to sleep. The call I always ignore (except if Lucy makes it) is something like, 'Come on Oliver, come on.' That sounds like an order to me and I am the one who should be giving those.

Day 216

I wasn't planning to be in the tree all day yesterday but the pair of large poodles who have just moved in next door spotted me and spent ages trying to climb up and harass me. But I knew they couldn't climb and I laughed at their hopeless efforts. Nevertheless, I was annoyed so decided I needed to work out how to let them know who is charge around here and why they shouldn't mess with Fish Tiger and his Tail.

But then I had a chat with Zinger who warned me that, 'Those big poodles are pretty bright you know, at least as far as dogs go. They're fast and nimble too; you'd be better off making friends with them – could be useful.'

So, I went back to the apple tree and the dogs came rushing out at me again.

'Good afternoon,' I said. 'I would like to welcome you to the area. It is very nice having such a handsome pair of dogs like you here now. Why, you must be the best-looking dogs around.'

The flattery seemed to work, as the dogs calmed down, wagged their nonsense tails and ran back into their house.

Day 217

Nan, Clint, Bubs and I all walked to the shops today. I wasn't supposed to come but as I had fallen asleep in the little compartment at the back of the stroller Nan hadn't noticed until we got there. We saw Margaret and we all went to her house for old fruity-smelling bottles for her and Nan, cake for Bubs and Clint, and fish for me. I put one of the fish from the pond in the back of the stroller and went home curled up with Bubs, purring in her ear to keep her from crying or telling anyone about the fish.

As we passed next door's house the poodles came out to say hello and I asked them if they liked fish. They said that they did – so I gave them my fish as a welcome present and they seemed very pleased with it.

Day 218

This morning Ron and Bruce, who have moved in next door, knocked on our door – with their poodles – and introduced themselves. 'I would invite you in,' said Richard, 'but the furry one here might be a bit worried about these guys.' To show that I wasn't, I jumped from Richard's arms onto the

ground and gave both the dogs a lick. They were pleased to see me and in seconds we were playing roughly but fairly, and I only had to swat each of them on the nose once to keep them in order. They are very big poodles and don't always know their own strength. They are already three times my size, but by the look of their paws they will be twice as big again.

Ron asked Bruce if we had a carp pond and explained that the dogs had come into the house last night with one. They wanted to find the owner to apologize and make amends. But as it was not us, they couldn't think where else it might have come from. Lucy joined us and gave me an unusual look but with a big smile. Lucy is so clever that she will have worked it all out and it will be our little secret.

Matilda and Martha are Standard Poodles, so Lucy said over dinner, and they are used as police dogs in some parts of Europe. They are very smart and can be trained. I went to sleep after dinner thinking what I could train them to do.

Day 219

No time for dogs or children today. There was a fresh mousehole in the hunting grounds. I watched it all day and did not see much movement, just one worried-looking mouse dashing in and shortly after that another one ran out.

I moved my face to the hole and my whiskers detected about five tiny babies in the hole. No wonder the parents looked so busy. I don't like to be unkind so I told them they had two weeks to leave and if they liked I could ask an owl to give them a lift out of my hunting grounds. They said that wouldn't be necessary, thank you, and blocked up the hole.

Day 220

Decided to zoom around all my territories today at very high speed. I was worried about a whole family of mice arriving without my knowing about it, and I could just imagine what Nameless would have to say about that.

'Vermin, that's cat's business, Oliver. You can't let them get away on you, can you now? There will be no end to it, will there? Know what I mean?'

I started indoors, going up, down, across, through, over, then down and up the territory Richard had built me. Lucy popped out of her door and grumbled that it was 'just five in the morning' but when a cat's got things to do, well, a cat's got things to do. But I jumped on her bed afterwards and gave her lots of kisses. Then I sprinted through the house a few times to make sure I hadn't missed anything. Tomorrow I will do a much more detailed check inside and will be looking underneath as well as on top of things. Today's mission was just a warning to anything that shouldn't be there that their time was up.

I had the same plan for the hunting grounds. Jumping over a fat, croaky frog was quite funny as he would normally be the one that jumps and would have been impressed by my style. The magpies were as rude as ever.

All the birds around here make a lot of noise in the mornings, and it was hard to hear myself think. So I slowed right down and made a surprise attack on a pile of old leaves. A rat ran out and disappeared into the hedge. I went in after him but I was too big and couldn't get through the hedge, and saw the rat running towards the big lettuce patch next door.

Day 221

Today I confined myself to the kitchen, covering every little bit of it. I cannot fit behind the fridge anymore, but I put my paw there just in case and nothing bit it, and nothing came out with it, so I think that's all in order. I walked across the top of the fridge and on top of all the shelves. There were few things put there by people that shouldn't be there, so I tidied them up by knocking them to the ground. That's when Richard came in and told me it was 3.30 in the morning. I looked at him as if to say, 'Do I look like I need a clock?' and carried on tidying the tops of shelves and cupboards with Richard's assistance. After I came down one level, Richard went back to bed so I went with him.

Day 222

I was woken up late in the evening by a very loud noise, which sounded like either Matilda or Martha crying. I rushed out to help and saw that their collars had accidently clipped into each other's. As each one tried to push the other dog away, the collars just got tighter and they panicked more. I have of course been taught by tough street cats about removing collars so I jumped between them and lifted the catch on one of the collars, which released them both. I was impressed with myself; I'd shown even more than my usual brilliance.

Matilda and Martha just about licked me to death in gratitude and I had to go right home and spend the next four hours cleaning myself. Dogs! Still Matilda and Martha now owe me a favour. I will collect on that one day.

Day 223

I heard Richard saying to Sophia that now I had settled down a bit it was safe to put the goldfish bowl back where it belonged rather than cluttering up their bathroom cupboard. I struck a mature, settled pose and pretended to be asleep. Suckers.

Day 224

They did it! The goldfish bowl is back on top of the bookcase, and I can reach it. But first I needed to go and check on those pesky mice. Then I had to complete a

detailed patrol of every nook and cranny in the house and thereafter patrol the hunting grounds. The thought of it all was a little overwhelming. I needed fish and spent the morning demanding it from Richard.

Richard is a bit slow in the head at times. I have tried to educate him about what I need to eat and even moved out when it was tin after tin and packet after packet, day after day, but he has not yet learnt. Well, if Lucy thinks that she can teach me how to paint or read poetry, Richard must be capable of learning some culinary decency. That, though, will have to wait because if I don't go and check on the mice they might get completely out of hand and there will be new holes everywhere.

Richard shared some of last night's dinner with me. I quite like beef, so that was all right. But Lucy said she was becoming a vegetarian and maybe I should too. I shudder at the thought.

Day 225

Unusually, Owl was still up and about this morning. He is, I must admit, a splendid creature (for a bird, anyway). As white as my socks and with a huge head. I was terrified of him when I was small, but nowadays, I think he is more interesting than frightening. However, it was hard pretending not to be afraid when he flew over and sat right next to me as I was surveying the mousehole. I was supposed to have been super stealthily hidden but he didn't take any notice.

'Had your breakfast yet, little puss?'

I nodded.

'Well, leave me to mine and I won't bother you, and these mice won't either.'

Day 226

Since Owl is taking care of the mice for me, it has become even more important to educate Richard properly about feeding me the good stuff. Lucy is normally a bit better, giving me wonderful things from her plate, but with her becoming a vegetarian that will not be enough anymore. I know I like the odd flower head, herbs and sometimes grass as much as the next cat, and I have already eaten most of the catnip, but I like my protein too. So I am going to devise some memorable messages for Richard. There will be a set of responses ranging from total appreciation to clear horror at the food being offered. They cannot be subtle, as it's Richard and it will take him a while to work it all out.

Day 227

I checked with Matilda and Martha to see what they did when they weren't given the food they liked. I know they can't hunt for it. Martha said that she always gets what she wants, and Matilda said everything was her favourite. Dogs must have a shocking set of taste buds. I asked what they would do if they don't get what they want. Martha said that was unlikely, but she would bark loudly and jump up and down from right to left. I asked what they would do if they wanted to show they really liked something they were given. Matilda said she would bark very loudly and jump up and down from left to right. I asked if that might be confusing, but they told me not to worry because they would just bark louder in any case.

Dogs are not very bright.

Day 228

I am writing the list of messages down here today so I can refer to them. As I am teaching Richard how to feed me properly, I need to be consistent and remember them myself.

1. Eating it all quickly and tidily, and kissing his fingers and rubbing against his legs, means 'That was exactly right, thank you.'
2. Doing the same but no kissing or rubbing means 'More please.'
3. Eating most of it at normal pace and not tidying up the plate means 'That was just about okay but it's not what I wanted.'
4. Eating some of it slowly and leaving bits of it all over the kitchen means 'Are you serious?'
5. Shaking my foot at it and yowling and nibbling a bit means 'Oh yuk.'
6. Tipping my bowl over, yowling and running out of the house with my tail at full height means 'You are just being cruel.'
7. Leaving it completely untouched means 'This is obviously not meant for me.'

Day 229

Sophia announced that 'an especially important person from work' was coming for dinner tonight. Unusually, Sophia was working in the kitchen herself, so I spent the morning supervising and tasting. It was all good, with lots of fish and nice creamy things.

This must clearly be an important person, so I am going to make sure he has an enjoyable time and comes back. He was introduced as 'Boss' and Boss is particularly good with a ping pong ball. I dropped one on his lap and he knew exactly what to do. He enjoyed himself a lot and every time I dropped the ball after batting it around, he picked it up and threw it.

Then the ping pong ball landed in the goldfish bowl.

Day 230

It's not fair. Just because Boss threw the ball into the goldfish bowl, I am being blamed for knocking the bowl over and it smashing and spilling water everywhere. Including over Boss.

I had to go and retrieve the ball, and yes, I did spend quite a lot of time looking for the fish as well. They looked remarkably interesting — shimmering red prey irresistibly flaunting themselves in front of me. But it is not my fault that a fish swam into my paws and fell into my mouth. I was just trying to scoop the ball up. Richard and Sophia both shouted so rudely and loudly at me that I turned around in fright and Tail and my back paws all got mixed up with the bowl, which crashed to the floor.

The fish tasted quite nice, so while everyone was fussing around Boss and clearing up, I found the other one. But Sophia took it away from me and locked me in Lucy's room. I couldn't even get out of the windows, so I had to sleep.

Day 231

Sophia came back from work today and gave me a pat and some wonderful things to eat. Boss so enjoyed himself that he wants to come again with a friend who likes cats and apparently wants to meet me. They will be lucky after the havoc of his last visit.

Clint and I watched cartoons on television this evening. Sometimes they are briefly interesting, especially when there are birds and cats involved. The birds are not like the ones outside, but they are easier to see at night.

There was even a mouse on the screen tonight; though Nan tried to distract me, I was determined to catch it. I made the big leap but it ran away, and I hurt myself on the outside of its big box. Nan said that I was a silly puss, but Clint laughed, which is a lovely sound.

Checked in on my dinner tonight. I gave Richard a 4 out of 10. I should have caught the mouse.

Day 232

We are all going down to the big place we rent in the country for a long weekend. I had to check what was inside all the open suitcases and make sure they had packed

Flippity Fish and the laser pointer. I went next door to tell Matilda and Martha that I was going away and delegated them my authority over the hunting grounds and the rest of the street. They are not very bright but at least they are big enough to scare off rabbits, rats and mice. Martha asked what they would do if they saw anything moving and Matilda suggested that they both bark. Martha thought that was the best idea that she had ever heard.

At least the food was better tonight, as Richard and Sophia were emptying the fridge. Gave Richard a 5.

Day 233

As we drove off in both cars Martha and Matilda barked their goodbyes and Owl flew over the car on her way to bed. We passed Zinger, talking to that dodgy black cat but they both waved their tails at me. We stopped outside Margaret's house to drop off some more things from the fridge and she came to the door.

Margaret was wearing something odd over her face. It was a nasty piece of blue and white cloth attached to her ears, which covered her mouth and nose. As Richard was getting out of the car he put one on as well.

They looked ridiculous. I meowed so that Margaret knew I was there and then meowed in protest at what they were wearing, and meowed in more protest as nobody was taking any notice of me. Lucy let me out of my carrier and Margaret picked me up. I didn't like her face cloth, though, I gather they are called masks, so I put my right paw underneath it and lifted it off her ear. Everyone laughed and soon we were on our way. Lucy explained that there was a big disease and every human had to wear a mask when they went out as the masks helped stop the disease.

Day 234

This disease sounds like it might be good news for me. Everyone must stay in their houses if they can and work from home. That means both Lucy and Sophia will be at home all the time. If everyone doesn't get grumpy and Richard keeps bringing food and fruity bottles back, we can have a lovely life.

Day 235

We had to go home after just one night in the rented house. Richard said it was because we were going to be staying home (they called it 'in lockdown') from midnight tonight for at least five days. Sophia, Nan and Bubs had already

gone home, and Clint and I were in the back seat. Richard was driving and Lucy was sitting next to him and pressing buttons on her phone.

There were lots and lots of cars on the road and many police officers putting up notices with their name on it right across the middle of the road. The officers waved at me as we drove past.

At home there had been an enormous delivery of food boxes. 'Well done, Lucy,' said Richard – which means that her magic phone buttons must have made those food supplies come. I am going to see if I can use those buttons too. Maybe there is a button combination especially for fish.

Day 236

Everyone spent a lot of time watching television today. It wasn't interesting, though. Not even a fish. There were serious, well-dressed people talking while sitting behind a desk and then people wearing hospital clothes talking and talking. Then there were some pretty pictures with red and blue lines going up and up.

Clint, Bubs and I didn't take much notice and played chasings through the house, and nobody minded. They haven't even unpacked all their suitcases, so I showed Clint and Bubs how to help them do that and we managed to put a lot of things on the floor.

I can sense that people are worried about the disease. I gave everyone extra kisses and attention, but all the adults were quieter than normal.

I spoke with Martha and Matilda, who said that they

were not worried about any disease coming and that they would just bark it away.

Day 237

Everybody got out of bed late today and they were all in their pyjamas watching television. They seemed pleased to see me, though. It was the same people and pretty lines going up on television, which I didn't think was very interesting. Neither did Clint, so we went around the hunting grounds today. We chased the magpies, and I was starting to teach Clint how to climb trees when Sophia called us in for breakfast.

It was very unusual, as everyone was sitting around the kitchen table at the same time, and Richard and Nan had prepared a big cooked breakfast. I think Lucy has forgotten that she has become a vegetarian as she didn't share much of her bacon with me, but Richard put some in my own bowl, and scrambled egg as well. I gave him a 2 for that.

Then, more amazingly still, everyone helped wash up the dishes and stayed around talking with each other. They normally just grunt and rush out. I had lots of laps to choose from and spent the day asleep on several of them.

Day 238

Everyone spent the evening watching *The Godfather* movies and I picked up some new ideas. I think I may find a new means of expressing my displeasure. I will work on a new number 8 for Richard.

Day 239

I went to see Matilda and Martha. They were happy that everyone was at home because of this disease but felt that five walks a day with Ron and Bruce was a bit too much. They asked if I had noticed how quiet everything was. I thought the opposite, as the birds seem to be getting louder, but Matilda said that was because there were only a very few cars and trucks on the roads as everyone is in lockdown.

Day 240

This lockdown is a very good idea. Everyone is much happier, and they all have more time for me and each other. I spent the afternoon in the kitchen, where Sophia and Richard were making jam. It was obvious they hadn't done it before, and they certainly needed my help. I did, though, nearly burn myself when I jumped onto the kitchen bench and took the tasting spoon just as Sophia was about to use it. Sophia just laughed and gave both Richard and me a hug.

Day 241

Lucy, Sophia and Nan were painting each other's toenails this afternoon. Well, the sight of all those toes was just too much. So I pounced on Nan's and gave her a playful little nip and hid behind the curtains. Then it was Lucy's turn, but I only gave her big toe a friendly, sloppy kiss and she laughed.

Sophia was harder game to catch. She has the most tempting toes as they are longer than anyone else's. I waited patiently for a whole minute then leapt in a big bound from underneath the curtains to where Sophia's toes should have been. But Sophia moved them just in time and picked me up for a tummy rub instead of being bitten. I was happy with that.

Day 242

There was fish for dinner and after giving Richard a 2, I had some more and gave him a 1. Need to sleep it all off.

Day 243

There was a strange man in my hunting grounds today. It was before anyone else was up. He had just climbed over the fence with a lettuce and some carrots and walked out in front of the house. Matilda and Martha must have been asleep as they didn't bark at all.

That man should at least have asked my permission and been polite enough to say good morning to me. I am worried about him. I don't like lettuce or carrots myself, and after the incident with the rabbits Richard has all that is needed for the kitchen, but I am sure the man wasn't paying for them.

Day 244

I went to have a chat with Zinger, who said that he was very hungry. He didn't really like vermin and lived off food from the street cart. But the disease had shut the cart down.

I expect the man in my hunting grounds was in a similar position. I took Zinger home with me; he was very familiar with cat flaps and I allowed him to eat all my breakfast, which Richard had already put out. Zinger then went to his normal places. It only took ten minutes to do that but Richard said that the kitchen smelt very strongly of cat and he asked Nan to give me a bath. I hate baths; they make me too wet and it takes me ages to clean myself properly afterwards.

Day 245

Richard and Lucy took turns today with the laser light. I had to pounce up walls, across bookcases, through cupboards and into the bath (while Bubs was in it), out of the cat flap and right through the garage and back. That thing didn't stop. It exhausted Richard and when Lucy took over it went upstairs, invading my special territory. I leapt, bound, climbed, jumped, scratched and flew but still it wouldn't give up. That light is a real demon. I was desperate but after one lightning-fast leap onto it, while it was on the lightshade overhanging the stairwell, Lucy caught me and told me that I had caught it.

Day 246

That odd black cat came right into my kitchen today. It was early in the morning. Richard had put the breakfast out but had just taken Sophia her coffee. I asked the cat what it was doing here.

'Zinger said it was all right,' the cat replied.

'It's my house, not his,' I said. 'Can't you get your own food?'

'Yes, but Zinger said your grub was really good and I am bored with mine.'

Then I remembered what had worked with this cat before. I rolled myself into a big ball, hissed and made a vertical take-off.

The black cat yowled and ran out the cat flap, and Richard and Sophia came charging in.

Day 247

There was a delivery this morning and Richard was keen to show me what it was. Lucy seemed excited too.

I am now wearing a new collar with what Lucy calls 'the magic magnet' built into it. Richard, who always likes banging things, was adjusting my cat flap. It seems that only my magic button can open it now. I am very happy that they want to stop invading cats but not sure about never being able to get rid of my collar.

Day 248

Zinger came around for breakfast again, but I explained why he couldn't come in.

'But old Blackie came in yesterday?'

I told him what had happened and suggested that if Zinger was still hungry he might go over to Blackie's instead, as he said he didn't like his food much so there was bound to be quite a lot left. Zinger thanked me. Before he left, he asked if I had followed his advice and made friends with the big poodles. Zinger didn't seem too pleased when I told him that we were known as Oliver's Mob and were bound by a secret code to be loyal to each other. Zinger said that I had been watching too much television and went on his way.

Day 249

My magic magnet works very well. I have been testing it all day, in and out, and it never fails.

I was so happy that I ran up a big tree to see if I could spot Matilda and Martha and share the news with them, but they didn't seem to be around. So I decided to go and see Margaret.

Margaret was home and her cat flap was open. I jumped on her lap and she seemed very pleased to see me. After a little play and some fish, she took me outside to show me her fishpond and there was a whole new big fence right around it now, far too high to jump over. I cannot think why she showed me this so I went into the house and slept on Margaret's bed.

Day 250

They tricked me this morning. Lucy and Richard were talking outside and invited me to join them. I thought they wanted a bit of company, so I happily ran over and right up Richard. From his neck I leaned over and dropped down onto Lucy. I was purring and everyone was happy. But then Lucy suddenly grabbed me tight and shouted out, 'Now, Dad!' Richard picked up the cat carrier he was hiding and threw me into it.

Worse still, we went off to the vet. That was as horrible as ever but soon over. I have not forgiven them for not telling me about the appointment. They didn't even give me time to hide.

Day 251

I still haven't forgiven them. But something did happen at the vet as I feel less itchy. It has been bad ever since Blackie invited himself into my kitchen and I am glad that I have not seen him since.

Lucy seems keener on having me back in her room. There

were quite a lot of new things to investigate, and I found her phone and padded on the numbers, as best as I could. Hopefully I have ordered some fish.

Day 252

Clint and I went for a race around the hunting grounds. We decided to run in a big loop but in opposite directions. Nan came out to watch and then Bubs came to join us. Nan shouted her support for Clint and Bubs, but I knew she wanted me to win as she picked me up and patted me every time I ran past her.

The magpies were watching as well and one of them came a little too close to Bubs, so I made an enormous leap and it flew away, grumbling that I was very rude. Well, a cat must protect the family.

Day 253

The fish still hasn't arrived. Lucy's phone is not working. She left it on again this morning with the numbers in plain view, so I had another attempt, but she stopped me after a funny sounding voice came out of it.

There was no fish in the kitchen either and Richard was lucky to get a 4 today.

Day 254

Since the disease appeared, Sophia and Richard have been spending much more time in what they call 'the garden' and what I know as the hunting grounds. They have their own ideas as to what should happen in my territory.

Today they were playing a game. There are a lot of small metal hoops. There are big different-coloured balls which can just fit through the hoops and a couple of painted sticks planted in the ground that the balls also must hit. The human players have a stumpy stick attached to a handle that they hit the balls with, which they call a mallet.

I didn't like where they put the hoops so I lifted them out and put them in more interesting places. Then I went inside and heard that we are all going to play 'croquet' tomorrow.

Day 255

We were all divided into teams for the croquet game: Nan and Richard, Sophia and Bubs, and Clint, Lucy and me.

Humans are normally very interested in rules, but it was very hard to work out what they are in this game. It quickly became clear that my job was to chase after every ball, other than the one Lucy's team hit, and push it as far away from all the hoops as possible. The ball that Lucy or Clint hit needed me to push it through the hoop they were aiming at. I also worked out that I had to push the wooden sticks as hard as possible away from everyone else's balls to stop it hitting the stick.

The game went on for so long that we stopped for lunch. I slipped out while nobody was looking and moved Sophia and Richard's balls well away and pushed ours right into the hoop.

After lunch everyone went a bit mad. Rather than get the balls through the hoops they started aiming at each other's balls and shooting them into the wilder areas. I had to rush there, move them further away and hide them. They still haven't found one so I suppose I will have to roll it back for them. It's Sophia's ball, though, and she hasn't been very nice to me today so I think I will wait.

Day 256

Richard is moving into the garden. He put what looks like a lot of small wooden walls down on the ground. Scratched his head a lot and went indoors for the night. I think he is trying to build a house. I went and put my mark on it.

Day 257

Sophia and Richard were up at first light this morning, digging up the ground near the wooden walls. I stood guard and scared the nosy magpies away. There was a lot of banging and Sophia shouted at Richard a lot. Then there was more scratching of heads. Lucy joined them and they all looked at her phone for a long time. Then they started again, and a very small house appeared. It has a door, shelves for me to sleep on, and a window I can climb through.

But I am still going to sleep in the house.

Richard was too busy today and he only earned a 5 for dinner.

Day 258

I spent the day in, on and around the shed. I didn't want any bird or any creature thinking that they can sit on it, hide around it or have anything to do with my new shed.

Later, Richard covered the shed with a stinky, dark fluid so horrible that I needn't worry about anyone using the shed at all. It was so smelly that I knocked over the big tin it was in. While Richard was clearing it up, Lucy came out and told me that she could go back to school tomorrow now that lockdown was over.

Day 259

The house was empty today. I had a big fight with the rude red cushions on the kitchen chair. They didn't give up easily, but they are now completely dead. Their stomachs were not very good to eat, though, so I just scattered them all over the kitchen.

Richard wasn't very happy when he came home. He asked if it had been snowing inside. That was a very strange thing to ask. I gave him a kiss and reminded him about dinner.

Nan came back with Clint and Bubs and more shopping than I have ever seen before. Clint thought the white cushion stuffing was fun to play with and covered Bubs and most of the house with it. So why am I the one in trouble?

Day 260

I found the goldfish food this morning. The goldfish don't need it anymore so I thought I would try it. It has an extraordinarily strong smell and tastes very rich – quite nice. I left some for Bubs.

Spent the afternoon eating grass and being sick.

Day 261

I walked Lucy back from the bus stop as usual. Why she thinks she needs to put me on the leash as soon as she gets off the bus is beyond me. I can clearly get to and from home and the bus stop without her help. However, Lucy is the cleverest human I have ever met and she may have reasons that I don't understand.

Everyone is still wearing masks but I was able to see clearly that Lydia was also on the bus, and although Echo isn't supposed to be distracted, I did see him wag his tail at me. Echo is such a wise dog; I do hope to see him again soon.

Day 262

It was windy last night and the shed fell over. It came down with a big crash so I rushed outside to help, and Richard and Sophia were already there. Richard was scratching his head and Sophia was waving her arms around and shouting. I jumped onto one of her waving arms, managed to stay on and clambered onto her neck and gave her a big kiss. Sophia was very happy about me being there and started to laugh. They went back indoors and left me to guard the remains of the shed.

Day 263

They didn't do anything about the shed so I was supposed to be there all day guarding it, but as lunch was late and only a 3 I went on strike and went to meet Lucy off the bus.

However, I got chased by a horrible big white dog, who said that he only wanted to play. But I was scared and ran home. Somebody had put an enormous blue plastic sheet over what had previously been the shed and I hid underneath it, and the dog tried to get in. He was very big and his snout lifted the sheet up just before I swiped his nose. He ran off but a gust of wind blew the sheet after him. I chased them both but the wind blew the sheet back and it landed on me.

I didn't know what I was fighting; I couldn't tell which was the sheet and which the dog. Then Richard and Lucy started playing peekaboo with me from both ends of the sheet. I do wish these people would take some situations more seriously.

Day 264

I went to see Matilda and Martha, who were practising synchronized jumping. This time Martha was jumping to the left and Matilda to the right. They said they were too busy to play with me but if I wanted I could give them a score for the quality of their jumps. I showed them what a real jump looks like and told them they had to get that high before they were worth judging. They tried but jumped into each other instead and that started a mock fight. I joined in but they are still a bit big for me, so I had to roll away and kept rolling all the way home.

Day 265

The seasons have changed, and I am glad that my fur is getting thicker. Lucy gave me a lovely comb-through tonight while she was pretending to play piano on my head. I am glad that cats don't multitask. It never seems to work well for humans.

I discovered a new word today: Builder. People get very excited and upset whenever they hear the word. Apparently, they are very hard to catch, but people put a lot of effort into it and then they escape before you have got them home. And, unlike mice, you cannot catch another builder if the one you are after has escaped. You have to finish with yours before taking on the next one. That's a very bad hunting technique. But Richard seems clear that finally he will bring one in over the doorstep tomorrow.

Day 266

Builder arrived. She came in a big white van with lots of interesting dents outside and boxes and things to explore inside. She has a funny way of talking and generally makes the same sort of noises Clint makes when he doesn't like his food. Builder's favourite sounds seem to be 'murrer', 'eurrg', 'narrrr' and 'jummrrrr', and every time she makes them Richard looks worried.

They were standing by what had previously been the shed when Builder pulled out her phone, tapped away on it and showed the screen to Richard. He waved his arms about and she did the same then tapped away again and made a noise something like 'bersrIcandddooo'. They shook hands and she drove off.

Richard looked at me and said, 'Tomorrow, puss.'

Day 267

Builder came and put a big bag next to the blue sheet then drove off. I climbed into the bag. There was nothing in there.

Day 268

Lucy and I stayed extra close last night. There was a huge storm. This morning there were lots of leaves on the ground in large piles capable of hiding something naughty. I had to pounce on all the leaf piles, but new ones kept forming. It was what I imagine catching fish from a big shoal feels like. The leaves kept moving and it was very tiring keeping them all in line.

I invited Matilda and Martha over to help. Their barking and synchronized jumping combined with my pouncing moved the leaves to completely cover the builder's bag and what was the shed. The big blue sheet must have blown away in the night.

Went back to Matilda and Martha's house and slept in their enormous basket. So did they, which was a bit of a squash but very warm.

Day 269

The food at Matilda and Martha's house is disgusting. I don't think dogs have any taste buds and they just seem to inhale their food. I remember that Bear did that as well. I am rather missing Bear and if he doesn't come soon I'll try and work out a way to get to him myself. I want to show him my new leaps and how much I have grown. I bet he has grown as well.

Day 270

Nan was asleep on the fat chair in the nursery, and I kept her company all day. I have worked out that from the top of the chair I can spring onto the base of the new mobile. But I don't think Richard would be very happy if another thing he constructed fell apart. On the other hand, those shiny objects moving around and around are very tempting. They must be prey.

Nan was still asleep when it was time for her to pick up Clint from preschool. I tried nudging, licking and headbutting her, but Nan just kept on sleeping. So, I decided I would have to go. Clint can walk well now so my plan was that he could follow me home.

The last time I was at the preschool I took careful notes of where Clint's classroom was, and today, I easily found my way in. There were a lot of happy children there, many of whom I had already met. The one adult there, the teacher, was writing things on a board so I jumped on her desk and faced the class as they sat on mats on the floor. They were all pleased to see me and even the teacher gave me a smile.

'It's Oliver!' shouted Roger and then they all took turns patting me. I did enjoy being the centre of attention and for a while forgot why I was there.

Lydia arrived with Echo, and I had to explain that I was there to pick up Clint. Echo was a little worried and didn't think Clint would be safe enough with only me as his protector and guide. I reminded Echo that it was not very far, but he said he would bring Roger and Lydia along too and then there would be five of us. That all worked, as Lydia is happy going wherever Echo goes, Roger too, and Clint enjoyed Roger's company.

Lydia and Nan were pleased to see each other, and Echo and I had a good catch-up. He gave me some useful advice about dealing with humans.

Not all the best animals are cats, and Echo is a very clever animal, so I am pleased to know him.

Day 271

Builder arrived with four friends. I didn't like the look of the friends. Two of them put smelly burning sticks in their mouths and they all looked very badly dressed. Builder was obviously upset about her empty bag being covered by leaves, but she shouldn't have left it there in the first place.

The five of them wandered around the remains of the shed, scratched their heads, burnt some more smelly sticks and played with their telephones. Then they suddenly all looked at their watches and drove off. They hadn't done anything other than pick up her bag and, worse still, they all ignored me.

Day 272

I hadn't even had breakfast when Builder and her friends arrived back in two vans. I have already been inside Builder's van but the other one seems even more interesting. There are lots of shelves and drawers, each one holding shiny things of assorted sizes.

I was just having a good sniff of a lunch box when suddenly a rough pair of hands picked me up and threw me not that gently out of the truck and onto the ground. I couldn't see who it was, but I saw his legs. He was shouting something too and I don't think it was about how great cats are. I was terribly upset, especially as a magpie saw it all and laughed at me.

Builder and friends didn't do anything today, as they all went off in her van as soon as it started raining.

Day 273

I was up early today and sure enough the nasty man's van was still there. He had closed the doors, but I manged to creep in and out of a little side window.

I found out that all those drawers came out easily enough so I tipped everything in all of them into a big pile on the van's floor. I was so excited I had to wee all over it.

Day 274

I went to see Matilda and Martha today. They were complaining that since lockdown was over Ron and Bruce only go walking with them twice a day.

I explained about Builder's friends and that I might need to collect a favour and Matilda barked and jumped to the left and Martha barked and jumped to the right so I know they will help.

Day 275

Rained again today. Just slept.

Day 276

It was a busy house today. Clint was playing with Roger, Bubs with Sophia, Richard with Nan. So Lucy and I went for a bicycle ride to the park. I was chased by some angry ducks who said that 'cats were not allowed'. I am glad they cannot run fast, and I was able to run around them in big circles. The ducks just quacked louder and louder, and then they all went into the lake. I am adding 'duck scaring' to my list of abilities.

Day 277

It hasn't rained for a day now, so Builder and friends came back. A big, smelly, stick-burning man swore and threw something at me, which missed. Richard saw it, though, and was very angry. He waved his arms around and the man just folded his arms. Richard pointed at the driveway, but the man just stood there. Builder came to see what the fuss was about and then stood there like the man with folded arms.

They then changed their minds and everyone, including Richard, walked to the remains of the shed.

I went to find Martha and Matilda and they quietly followed me to the building area.

Each of Builder's four friends was holding up one of the four small walls. Builder was connecting them. The man who attacked me had one hand on his wall while the other held a smelly stick. I got closer. Then closer. Then I leapt on his legs and bit one. He yelped and dropped his wall, which hit Builder, who fell over and knocked down the connecting wall. Martha and Matilda barked into action, which added to the chaos, and the remaining walls fell over, narrowly missing Builder.

Ron and Bruce came running to see what the fuss was about. Builder stood up as did her friends. They looked angrily at me, but Matilda and Martha barked louder and jumped higher. Richard was laughing and Builder found it too difficult and they all just left.

Ron and Bruce looked at the remains of the shed, went home for a few things and then finished the job with Richard, so by the end of the afternoon the shed was securely up.

Day 278

Ron and Bruce came for dinner tonight, as did Martha and Matilda. They are all family friends now. I am still super happy about our victory. Richard didn't have to pay for the shed to be rebuilt so the family has been enriched. Martha and Matilda have proven that they are good enforcers. I have somewhere new to sleep and Oliver's Mob has again demonstrated its invincibility.

Day 279

I have been thinking about what to do with the mice and remembered that I need to get one for Richard. I must be very careful not to damage it, so he gets to see an example in perfect condition.

Day 280

Owl got to the mice first. She is going to have babies soon and needs all she can eat. Richard will have to wait.

Day 281

The bridge over the stream is beginning to fall over. I need the bridge as I hate getting my feet wet and the stream is too big for me to leap across. Somehow, I should let Ron and Bruce know about it as they are very good at fixing things. I need a plan.

Spent the day admiring my white socks.

Day 282

I went to see Margaret today, who needed to play with the ping pong balls for about an hour. There are a few fish left in her pond, so I am sure she won't miss a couple. But the fence around it looks difficult to get through; I do wish I was stronger.

Day 283

Yesterday on the way back from Margaret's I ran into Zinger, who was pleased to see me. He said that he wanted me to know more about cat lore. So I invited him for breakfast today, but he couldn't get through the cat flap. We eventually worked out that if I held it open from the inside he could just squeeze in. But Richard saw us.

Seeing that Zinger and I were friendly, Richard gave him a special food bowl all to himself. Zinger has good manners and thanked Richard by rubbing against his legs. Richard looked for his collar, but Zinger doesn't have one.

Zinger and I spent a few hours on the bridge while he told me lots of stories, including the tale of a cat who lost his tail and spent years trying to find it. The tail was found but it was on another cat and a fearful fight ensued.

I think Zinger must have made that up.

Day 284

Spent today thinking about Zinger's stories. He must have made them all up. But I do hope the story of how the

Egyptians used to look after cats is true. Maybe when I am very big I will travel to Egypt, wherever that is. Meantime, today is Monday. It's the only day that Margaret doesn't eat fish and she makes the most beautiful diced chicken livers so I am going there to help her eat them.

Day 285

Last night's dinner was superb. Today the boring stuff from a tin, again, that Richard gave me deserved the 4 I gave it. But I hid in the laundry cupboard in case he disagreed. Nan has been trying to organize this cupboard, but I think she should have another go to make it more comfortable. I helped her to get started by pushing everything from the cupboard onto the floor. I tried to do it so everything fell in size order, but I don't think I manged it that well. Nan came in and just shook her head at me so I probably could have done a better job — but at least I tried to help.

Day 286

Sophia was in the kitchen all day today. Boss is coming back for dinner tomorrow with his 'friend who likes cats'. I think I'd better be calm and behave well.

I tested some of the smoked salmon and the cream. They are a marvellous combination; I don't understand why they don't serve it like that. I am looking forward to tomorrow night's dinner. Sophia picked me up and said, 'I wonder what we should do with you, puss, after last time?' The cheek of it! It's not my fault that I had to retrieve his ball from the

goldfish bowl where he had thrown it.

I was upset by Sophia's unreasonable attitude so I wriggled free and went back into the kitchen. Sophia had forgotten to put the rest of the smoked salmon away, so I saved her the trouble.

Day 287

Boss's friend is as big as a mountain. He is called Gerrard and has a beard which hangs all the way from his chin to his lap. I don't normally like beards and sometimes I am not sure about the men who hide behind them. But Gerrard's beard smelt nice, rather like the woods near our holiday place.

Boss was friendly to me as well, and Gerrard had me on his lap for most of the evening, so I was able to straighten out his beard. Gerrard lives with his wife, who is supposed to be allergic to cats so he cannot invite any into his home. Now that's a sad thing.

After I had helped Sophia clean the plates I went to sleep on Gerrard's lap. He must have moved me very gently because I didn't wake up until the early hours of the morning.

Day 288

The second Clint opened the door this morning, Bear came bounding in and knocked him over and started licking him. Clint laughed.

'What kind of dog is that?' asked Richard, and Bella told him that Bear was a Labrador Huntaway Cross. They have come to stay for a whole week, and everyone is very pleased to see them.

Day 289

Bella decided that as a way of thanking Sophia and Richard for letting her stay for so long, she would prepare the dinner tonight. It was marvellous (or at least I thought so). Tuna and yoghurt, albeit with annoying green things. Richard, Nan and Sophia said that it tasted tremendous, but they could not eat everything on their plates as Bella had given them too much.

I cleaned up the plates.

Day 290

Bear came and woke me up this morning, complaining that we hadn't had much fun yet, so I took him over to Martha and Matilda's. They had a very big barking competition, and it was just as well that Bruce and Ron were out. But then I had an idea about the bridge.

I told all three dogs that they were each excellent at

barking but that there could only be one chief barker. I was prepared to judge a barking competition tomorrow morning before the humans had left for the day. The winner would be known as the Oliver's Mob Barker-in-Chief.

Day 291

I woke all the dogs up just after first light and led them to the bridge, which I told them was the ideal place for a competition as the acoustics were superb. I have learnt that dogs believe anything.

Bear started off but he wasn't all that loud — though he was loud enough to bring Bella and Lucy out looking for him. Then Martha had a go, and she was clearly louder than Bear. Then Matilda was louder still, and her barking brought Nan and Richard running to join Bella, Lucy and me on the bridge. I then asked Matilda and Martha to bark together competitively. That very quickly had Ron and Bruce also running onto the bridge. The bridge collapsed under the weight of everybody just a second after I had jumped clear of it.

Day 292

Ron and Bruce spent the morning fixing up the bridge and Richard said that they and Martha and Matilda were welcome to use it to go into the woods any time they liked.

The Oliver's Mob infrastructure has been improved and our friendships widened. Another success!

Day 293

I was walking into the kitchen this morning when a giggling Bubs ran past me. She can walk and run all by herself now. In some ways the speed with which humans develop is, compared to cats, extraordinarily slow but it's still good to see it happen.

Bubs, Bear and I spent the day running outside. I am a lot faster, and she trips up, but she will become a worthy competitor. That is, if she ever stops giggling. Bear just keeps on going whatever happens.

Nan came to find us, and we played hide and seek in the woods. Except Nan didn't know that was what we were playing and was cross with us when Bubs and Bear surprised her by running out of the stream.

Day 294

Clint and Bubs were having a squabble today. There was some pulling and pushing and Bubs way crying, and Clint was red in the face trying not to cry. Bear and I had to provide the necessary distractions quickly.

Bear thought it was a good idea to push me over and

show Clint how easy it was for bigger things to knock over smaller ones, and that it wasn't always a good idea. Clint laughed when Bear did that, but I manged to roll away underneath Clint's feet and trip him up. Bubs thought that was very funny and jumped on top of us all.

At that moment, Sophia came into the room.

Day 295

Bear disappeared this morning for a short time but came back into the hunting grounds covered in chicken feathers. I knew there would be trouble and quickly invited Martha and Matilda over and took them inside.

The scarecrow man came back with his dogs and banged on the door, and Bear, Matilda and Martha restarted their barking competition. The scarecrow's Rottweilers didn't join in; rather, they dragged him away. Like before, he then came back with his wife. Somehow, Bear had discovered their chicken coop and charged into it. Luckily, there was no damage caused.

Richard explained that Bear was only visiting, and he would be kept secure until he left tomorrow evening.

Day 296

As soon as it was light, Bear showed me where the chickens lived, and we spent the morning salivating. Bear likes chicken, but not as much as I do. However, the chicken that both of us eat doesn't look anything like those daft two-legged creatures in their cages.

Then it was time for Bear to go home, and I was very sad to say goodbye. Unlike many cats, I have several dog friends, but Bear is my favourite.

Once Bear had gone, the chickens were too big for me to tackle alone, so I decided to come back and spend another day trying to work out how to convert these birds into necks, livers, thighs and breasts.

Day 297

I summoned up the courage to get myself right outside the chicken coop and saw that they had chicks. They are very cute. I went into the coop and made friends with them. I was asleep with a few chicks when the rooster woke me up and asked me very politely to do some work around the place. There were mice and rats everywhere.

I made sure that all the chicks were safely in the back of their cage. I then told Rooster to get all the big ones under cover and I went to find Owl.

Owl has had babies now and was very keen to hear of a new mice supply.

Day 298

Between us, Owl and I took care of the mouse problem. Owl told me that I was a good friend to her family. But she said she wasn't vaguely interested in rats and wouldn't know what to do with them anyway. So to get rid of them from the coop, I would have to fight one myself.

The fight was nasty and dirty. I chased the rat into the

barn, and he turned around and reared up, about to swipe me. I bashed him across the face and pounced on him, but he fought himself free and ran up the wall. I followed him then leapt on top of him and, grappling each other, we both fell to the ground. But the rat hit his head on the concrete floor, and I bit his neck and started looking for the next one.

But there were too many.

Day 299

Nameless was very pleased that I seemed to have got into the vermin business and was honoured to help when I asked. I didn't tell him about Owl and the mice, but he took care of the rest of the rats, taking a big one back for Lolly.

I went back to sleep with my new chick friends and was woken up by the scarecrow man and his wife. They seemed pleased to see me. They had worked out that all by myself I had removed all their mice and rats, and that their chicks and eggs were now safe.

This evening the scarecrow man came to the door and left a big box of eggs for us and a nicely prepared pile of chicken that looked like it was ready to eat.

Day 300

This was a successful week. The family's provisions have increased. There are more people, cats, birds and animals obliged to us and the territory of Oliver's Mob has extended to include a whole farm. There will be much work to do there, so I think it might be time to re-billet Lolly and Nameless.

The last time I saw him, Nameless said that he was ready for a change. However, Owl might not be too happy about it so I will talk to her first.

Owl said she was surprised that I was hanging around with 'down-market mousers' and that I should think about making more upscale friends. Owl is right and I will leave Nameless and Lolly alone.

Day 301

On my way to see Margaret I was nearly knocked out by the most amazing waft of food smells. The heavenly aroma was coming from a restaurant on the other side of the road. A man in a chef's hat saw me stop and very kindly invited me over. He put a warm bowl of shrimp, cream, prawns and white fish in front of me and kept watch while I ate it all. This man is a prince among gentleman, and I rubbed right up against him to show my appreciation.

The chef invited me inside for a moment. I was shocked to see another cat sitting on top of an open cupboard full of plates and wine bottles. He was an excessively big, blue-eyed ragdoll cat. He was quite the plumpest cat I have ever seen.

'Don't mind me,' he said. 'I have had far too much to eat, as usual, and anyway I'm too old to care much about territory nowadays.'

I wished him a good afternoon and complimented him on his choice of home. There are not many cats that are smart enough to get themselves digs in a fish restaurant.

'Quite right, young man. My name's Flutter, you know,

and I already know about you, Oliver. Quite the business with that tow truck bully you had. You are the kind of cat we like having around here, so do come back. If you like chowder, come on Sundays; it's creamy then. See you soon. I'm going back to sleep now.'

Day 302

When I got back to the house everyone was around the kitchen table and there was a quiet and unusual atmosphere. I jumped onto Lucy's lap to find out what was going on.

As far as I understood it, Nan was finding managing Clint, Bubs and much of the housework rather too much work. Lucy needed to concentrate more on her school work so couldn't help much more, and Richard was busy enough as it was. But nobody could work out what to do. Something had to change. It was obvious to me what needed to happen. There is plenty of room in our house and Margaret is lonely – perhaps she could move in with us to help Nan, when she wasn't at her job. But how could I get across the idea that she should come and live here?

Day 303

I went to visit Margaret. She has a distinctive, small pink scarf she wears around her head. While she was having an afternoon nap, I undid it and took it home and dropped it on Sophia's pillow.

Sophia came home and when she went into her bedroom, she came out angry and shouting at Richard. She dragged him into the bedroom and showed him the scarf. I jumped on top of it and meowed and meowed and rolled on top of the scarf and oofed at it.

Lucy came in and saw me and the scarf and said, 'Yeah, isn't that what Margaret wears?'

I really don't know what would happen to this family without Lucy. She immediately got the idea and explained it to Richard and Sophia. Margaret is coming for dinner tomorrow.

Day 304

I found Zinger and Blackie on the street this morning. They told me they were going on a roaming adventure across to the other side of town and asked if I wanted to come. I explained that I would be free to come in several days' time and we agreed to meet up on Tuesday evening.

Margaret came for dinner and there were plenty of pats for me, some good roast beef and even a creamy dessert. They got through lots of fruity bottles. The top of one of the fizzy ones blew off and I had to leap after it. I missed, but my dazzling efforts were applauded as I landed in the kitchen sink.

Day 305

I need to work out my days of the human week. My schedule is becoming pressured.

On Sundays, it's chowder at Flutter's.

On Mondays, chopped liver at Margaret's unless she comes and lives here.

On Tuesdays, Richard serves me up all the leftovers or tinned stuff.

On Wednesdays, the fish van comes.

On Thursdays, it's nearly always just stuff from tins.

On Fridays, Sophia often brings people over for dinner. Yummy food.

On Saturdays, there are leftovers from Friday night.

So, it seems that I still have Tuesdays and Thursdays free.

Day 306

Today proved to be a Thursday. I gave Richard a 4 and flounced off.

Day 307

Margaret came for dinner again tonight and had a long, private chat with Sophia, Richard and me.

Clint started crying in the nursery and very quickly Margaret went off to get him. Margaret came back a few minutes later with Bubs sitting on her neck and Clint holding her hand. I noticed that both Clint and Bubs looked

a bit glossier and smarter than normal, and that Margaret
looked happier than I have ever seen her.

After dinner Nan came in and seemed to be very happy to
see Margaret, and with the children too.

Day 308

Margaret stayed the night, and I helped her settle in and
kept her bed warm. But she did tell me to leave her scarf
alone. Margaret stayed all day and played with the young
ones while Nan slept.

Day 309

I had a lovely chat with Flutter today, who told me where all
the good nearby restaurants were. He was right about the
chowder — it was extra creamy.

The chef was as delightful as ever. After I had finished
and washed myself up, he introduced me to some of his
customers, all of whom were very sleek and well dressed
like the sort of people Sophia brings home. Some of them

were very messy eaters and there was quite a lot of fish that I needed to clean up from the floor.

On the way home I went, on Flutter's recommendation, to have a look at the Straight Pole, a famous restaurant apparently. But there was already a rabble of cats outside the back, and I was too full to want to fight my way in.

Day 310

There was chopped liver at Margaret's house as usual and I stayed overnight. Now that we are sharing responsibilities for my family, Margaret and I need to stay close.

Day 311

It's Tuesday and as the food at home is variable I think it's a day I can do what I want and I set out to find Zinger and Blackie. I crossed the park, dodging children and nasty little yapping dogs. One of them was a little persistent so I jumped at it, and she ran away yelping. I am a big cat

nowadays, to be taken seriously. But cutting through the hospital grounds I was over-confident and nearly had a calamity.

I was in unsafe open ground when I stopped to look at a mousehole in a grass bank. An enormous grey Weimaraner dog suddenly hurtled out of nowhere. I am fast over a short distance, but Weimaraners are fast too, and over longer distances. I could smell his breath as he was right on my tail. Then he bashed me with his head, and I went flying but landed well and turned around ready to fight. Fortunately, I didn't need to.

The officer guard dog from the hospital had seen the action and, barking orders to the Weimaraner to stop, he came running over. He told the Weimaraner that I was a protected member of the hospital team and not to be touched. This time he said he was letting the Weimaraner off with a warning but he would be sent to the pound if he ever approached me again.

Feeling relieved, sore and battered at the same time is confusing. The officer guard dog kindly took me to Mary's floor and found a bed for me to recover until Richard could pick me up.

Day 312

Today was fish van day and, though I was feeling guilty about not seeing Zinger and Blackie, I thought I deserved a day at home and was sure they would understand. Slept for most of the day but have just come back from checking on my chicks, which, though a little bigger, are still very fluffy.

Day 313

I am feeling a lot better today and, as it's yucky food day at home, I went off to find Zinger again. I was walking quietly down the road when Lucy pulled up on her bicycle and offered me a lift, which I accepted. Neither of us knew where the other one was going, but I decided that when she started going the wrong way I would jump out.

We hadn't gone very far when she stopped at the Straight Pole. Lucy was meeting a girlfriend for lunch. So I jumped out of the bicycle basket into Lucy's big bag. Flutter was right again: the food was magnificent. Lucy's friend didn't turn up but I was happy to console her and help eat her steak sandwich. I left her all the fries. After all, she should have been eating them, like a good vegetarian.

Went home with Lucy.

Day 314

Lucy was at school, so I spent the day with Richard. He needed reminding that my first birthday is coming up soon and that some incredibly special food will be required — and a lot too.

Richard picked me up after breakfast (which scored a 2) and asked, 'So when did you get so interested in food, not-so-little one?'

The cheek of it. Okay, I am super furry, sleek and fluffy but compared to Zinger I am positively big. Rotund was the word Zinger used. He came by to see why I hadn't joined their roaming party. I explained about the

Weimaraner, and my rescue one day and the fish van on another. Zinger was impressed. 'You've got real cool connections, Mr Oliver — you are a cool cat.' But Zinger sniggered about the fish van. Well, what would a common mouser understand?

Day 315

Margaret, Clint, Bubs and I spent the day watching Donald Duck and Mickey Mouse cartoons on television. I have already learnt that I need to be wary of ducks, but that mouse is ridiculous. I went off to find Nan and picked up her Goldwing's keys and dropped them on her bed. It was time she got up and did something.

Nan took me with her in my carrier and we zoomed through the streets, overtaking everyone. We heard sirens and saw some flashing lights, but Nan just went faster and faster and they left us alone. Nan took me to a fish restaurant; well, it wasn't exactly Flutter's and they didn't even have plates, but the fish was excellent. The ladies behind the counter were Lucy's age, but not as nice, though one of them gave me a tummy rub and a little bit of fish that

had not been battered, which was a lot easier to eat.

We came home through streets I had not seen before, and Nan had the Goldwing's lights off.

Day 316

Two policemen were at the door this morning asking to see Nan. Richard told them that she was asleep and they should come back this afternoon, and they agreed a time. Just before they came, Gerrard and his beard came back, and we were both incredibly pleased to see each other.

Gerrard is a lawyer, an exceptionally good one, and he persuaded the police that there was no glory in prosecuting a septuagenarian motorcycle hooligan.

While Gerrard was doing that, I was able to get inside the police car. It was smelly and loud, with lots of screens and radios cackling. I pressed and pushed all the buttons I could. Finally, the siren went off. I slipped away and the police officers came running back. One of them raced into the hunting grounds and the other ran down the street looking

for the person who had been in their car. Gerrard came out, laughed and picked me up, saying, 'Well done, puss.'

Day 317

Nan has decided to sell her Goldwing and Lucy took lots of advertising photographs with me sitting on it. I will be interested to see what kind of person is going to want to buy the motorcycle. I hope they don't think that I come with it.

Day 318

Zinger, Blackie and I found the Lemon and Thyme restaurant. Flutter had told me that they produced a most excellent beef bolognese sauce. I couldn't find the place alone, though, so had to share the secret with the others. We all washed ourselves up and, looking our finest, announced our arrival at the back door. A very happy-looking lady approved of our reservation and let us in, and we dined most superbly. We showed our gratitude and appreciation in the normal way by going to sleep on her chairs, and were gently shown the door a couple of hours later.

Day 319

Life is getting better, with at least five quality meal days built into my timetable now, but I need one more, so I set off to find the Slug and Lettuce. Flutter assured me that, despite its very unpromising name, they have the best steak and kidney in the whole area.

I had not been into one of these places humans call pubs before. It smelt of beer, steak and kidney. There were no dogs inside and, as I cautiously put my nose through the door, I saw a very welcoming place. Shiny glasses, joyful people, polished wood walls and tables and a dark floor. The man behind the counter gave me a smile and put a little saucer of water next to a safe window ledge overlooking the road. The view was exciting, as the entire world was walking by.

I needn't have worried about the food either, as soon a nice warm plate of steak and kidney arrived. It was very satisfactory indeed.

I introduced myself to all the customers, most of whom were incredibly pleased to see a cat. One of them ignored me, so I went to sleep on his lap.

Day 320

I have eaten far too much recently and needed all day to sleep and digest.

Day 321

Spent the day playing tiddlywinks with Bubs, Nan and Clint. Bubs and I were on the same team, and we won. That may be because whenever Nan and Clint flicked, I caught and hid their counters. Even Clint called me a daft cat and enjoyed himself. I am immensely proud of how Clint is becoming a very proper young boy. I still have lots

to teach him, but he is made of good things.

Sophia and Richard joined us in the afternoon and Sophia won. Well, she would, wouldn't she?

Spent the evening watching 'mega music hyper zoopery mix' with Lucy, who is teaching me how to dance.

Day 322

Bubs is becoming as pretty as Lucy, but she giggles much more. We went to the stream together today. Bubs was trying out what various kinds of mud looked like on her clothes, and I was hunting fish.

Margaret joined us and laughed so loud I thought she would fall over. Bubs was thrilled to see her and ran straight into Margaret's arms and her nice white dress.

Day 323

Tomorrow is my birthday; I am still not incredibly old, but I am definitely a big cat. I have powerful friends and influence and lots of places to get proper food. I am a proven killer, runner, planner and all-round feline masterpiece, and my modesty knows no bounds.

But despite all this, the
best thing ever – and
what truly matters more
than anything else – is
being in Lucy's arms.